NO ZOMBIES PLEASE WE ARE BRITISH

ALEX LAYBOURNE

SEVERED PRESS
Hobart Tasmania

NO ZOMBIES PLEASE WE ARE BRITISH

This is for my wife Patty and our five wonderful children, James, Logan, Ashleigh, Damon and Riley.

CHAPTER 1

Jack fished a crumpled twenty out of his back pocket and handed it over to the waiting employee of the local pizza place, all the while balancing the extra-large pepperoni and mushroom pizza in his other hand, and trying his hardest not to stare at the moustache.

As far as facial hair went, it was not a spectacular affair, certainly not Kurt Russell in *Tombstone* quality, but it was far from being a pencil-thin fifties movie star look. It was simply a decent moustache of relatively dark colouration.

The reason he didn't want to stare was because it adorned the face of a rather large woman, with dark eyes and a less than cheery disposition.

Jack was a somewhat regular customer at the local pizza parlour, and seemed to, more often than not, get stuck dealing with the moustachioed Amazon, who was taller than he was and certainly twice as wide.

He was sure that a strong correlation existed between her mood and the length of her facial hair, which never seemed to be trimmed or tamed in any way. He just never had been drunk enough to build up the bravado to ask her about it. Which was saying something because he had made more than his fair share of shit-faced takeaway calls over the years.

Twice he had woken up in bed hugging a pile of paper wrappings that smelled like the backside of a cow after a rather nasty stomach complaint. Wandering to the bathroom to find slices of salad and meat plastered over his face, and a headache more than worthy of the name threatening to tear his skull apart and leak its inebriated contents over the floor.

The woman fisted him his change and grunted her approval at his tip. Jack closed the door and went back to the living room. His girlfriend was away for a long weekend with her mother in the city, and his roommate was also out for the night. That suited Jack to the ground, because it meant pizza and video games. He had more than enough beer in the house to keep himself refreshed through the evening, and with the fifteen-inch pizza there to fuel him into the early hours, Jack was set.

He sat back, grabbed a slice and chomped off the end third. It was hot and gooey, the cheese dribbling over the sides, just the way he liked it. He downed the rest of his beer and let out a satisfied belch.

With the first slice inhaled, and a nice buzz growing, Jack returned to his video games. An ultra-violent third person sort set in a futuristic world laid low by a genetically engineered super virus. He had only bought it the previous day and was already engrossed in the world he was thrust into.

By the time Jack passed out on the sofa, it was the early hours of the morning. A pile of beer cans laid in the large pizza tray. The television was on soft, the midnight movie of the week playing.

At twenty-two, Jack was living the dream life, or so his youth convinced him. An athletic build, combined with an appetite that could never be suppressed and a metabolic rate that seemed off the charts, he was the envy of all his friends. His liquor consumption brought them back onto a level playing field. It didn't take much for Jack to get hammered, although he was proud of his repeated demonstrations of intestinal fortitude. He would not stop until everybody else did, which had been responsible for many drunken incidents he would rather forget but somehow just couldn't. Drinking had robbed him of many memories, but stupidity seemed immune.

Fresh out of university and with his own freelance software engineer business blooming, he laughed at those stuck in the

Monday to Friday rat race. His girlfriend, Sarah Welch, was twenty-one and in her final year of university. She had plans to become a teacher, and had the patience of a saint, as often demonstrated with her ability to tolerate Jack and his often immature antics.

They had been together for almost two years, and while they were committed to one another, they had never had any conversation pertaining to anything deeper or more meaningful.

Like Jack, his roommate, Terry, was a similarly immature man, but only on the weekends. During the week, he was a pencil pusher for a local business. It was a job he hated every minute of but suffered through, much to Jack's delight. All of it was done in order to earn enough to keep his girlfriend happy. A harsh featured, cold-eyed woman who had the personality to match. In the three painful years Terry and Sue had been dating, Jack could not remember seeing her smile. Terry spent the majority of his time trying to think of ways to avoid her, yet whenever Jack mentioned the notion of dumping her, Terry would get quite mad.

Jack didn't understand why. His roommate was not the most attractive guy on the market, but he was far from being the bug-eyed monster you would find discarded on the market floor at the end of the day. He would be more than able to bring home a fit enough bird on the weekends, make her scream once or twice and then get rid of her, but the man seemed totally against the idea. Preferring to suffer with a sexually frigid woman who made spinsters around the world seem warm and fuzzy.

The fact the Jack had once walked in on her while she was coming out of the shower, and he had made a passing comment about handing her a weed whacker to help contain the shrubbery, thus irritating Sue beyond belief, had possibly played a role in her disapproval of him. While her inability to take a joke was in itself close to being one.

Still, it was not him that risked getting frostbite every time he boned her, so what did it matter.

Jack woke with a start. He was still on the sofa. His neck was on fire; stuck and stiff from how he had passed out. His head had a gentle ache to it, nothing terrible, but enough to be noticed. Jack was not sure why he was suddenly yanked back into the conscious world, but his still being on the sofa was a strange affair. Normally, he would have woken, or been woken by Terry when he got home. Still, maybe Terry had stayed out, booked himself into a hotel, dumped Sue, and hooked up with a waitress while in some drunken stupor.

A police siren wailed, but again, living in North London, that was no strange sound. The house was silent, outside it was dark and grey. A disorienting light permeated through the thick cloud base. It could just as easily be late morning as it could early.

Jack looked around, unable to shake the heavy knot from his stomach. It was a little after eight in the morning, according to the clock in the corner of the television.

Looking out of the window, Jack saw nothing that caused any alarm bells to ring. It was a Sunday, so the streets would be quiet; the weather also doing nothing to encourage folk out of their beds. Yet the silence seemed strange, almost too much.

"There's a storm coming," Jack said to himself as he tidied up the remains of the previous night's binge.

Jack didn't believe it, but it was what his grandmother had always said to him on the very same type of dark and gloomy mornings.

Jack drank his coffee, checked the flat to make sure he was alone, and then took a shower. He hoped that would wash away the lingering feeling of ominous portent that seemed to be following him like a cloud in a cartoon.

Dressed and relatively confident that the hour was acceptable for phone calls, he tried to contact Sarah. He did so because she was his girlfriend, and he was interested in hearing how the show had been. Sarah's cousin, one of her closest friends, was a dancer in the West End production of *Thriller Live*. Sarah and her mother had gone to the city together to watch the show, which was in the opening week of its second run.

The phone connected, but there was no answer. He tried again and left a voicemail message, but half way through it, the phone cut out. Trying for a third time, sure that if Sarah was somehow still sleeping, his good intentions would see him firmly placed in her bad books ... but nothing.

Looking at the screen, Jack was confused by the lack of connection. The words 'No Service' were emblazoned across the screen.

The knot in Jack's stomach turned to ice. He turned on the television and flicked through the news channels. They all spoke about the same thing. Riots had broken out in the city. Information was scarce, but helicopter footage showed hordes of people running around the streets, buildings being looted, cars broken and overturned. Small fires burned in some residential areas. The images were short and fleeting, yet their impression was powerful. The message behind them was simple: Stay inside, and do not go into the city.

Under most circumstances, that would have suited Jack to the ground. He disliked the city, especially during the weekend, and staying in was not a problem. He had plenty of games to keep him entertained, as well as several projects he needed to start working on.

But it was not any other Sunday. There was something going on, and it didn't sit well with him.

Outside, Jack heard a commotion. A group of people were in the street. They were running, but not an out-for-a-jog-in-our-designer-tracksuit kind of run. It was a run of terror. *Fleeing* was the word that came into Jack's head.

In the street, someone screamed. From his third floor apartment, Jack watched the crowd disappear, the dense atmosphere of the day and the approaching sirens swallowing their cries and shouts of panic.

The view from his apartment was of a moderately busy road, which had a roundabout to the left and a crossing to the right. Both were visible from the apartment, depending on which room you were in and how far you were willing to crane your neck.

Two streets over there was a park. From the living room, it was possible to make out a small sliver of green through the gap between the A and B block of apartments on the opposite side of the street.

Jack looked around, trying to spot what had caused such panic. That was when Jack saw the woman lying face down in the middle of the road. He watched her for a moment, but she didn't move. Nobody came to her aid, and so he turned and sped from the flat.

He took the stairs down; they were far more reliable than the lift. Bolting two at a time, the voice inside his head was chirping to him. *Something is wrong. Something is definitely very wrong.*

Jack reached the ground floor and stepped out onto the street. The bare concrete steps that led to his building's door were as cold as ice. It was then Jack realized he was not wearing any shoes. It had started to rain, fat drops falling slowly but with the promise of an increased tempo.

The woman was still lying in the street. Her legs were moving, kicking as if she were trying to swim through the tarmac. The eerie whispering echo of screams and panic hung in the air, but Jack paid it no mind. He just wanted to check on the woman, call an ambulance if needed. He wasn't looking for trouble.

"Miss? Miss, are you okay?" he asked.

The woman gave no discernible answer. She gargled something, but the words were swallowed up by the road. She was wearing a long-sleeved black top and a tartan skirt, which had been pushed up during whatever scuffle had led to her current predicament. The curve of her ass cheeks could be seen beneath the pair of fishnet tights that covered her legs.

"Excuse me, Miss?" Jack tried again.

Crouching down, he placed a hand on the woman's shoulder. He could feel her body shaking. Pulling gently, he tried to roll her over. At first, she resisted, her body heavy in spite of her slight-looking frame. She rolled over and groaned. She looked at Jack, her vivid green eyes stared at him. Jack felt his world spin out of control. He cried out and fell backwards as he saw the woman's face.

The skin had been removed, and a large chunk of flesh had been removed from the left cheek. Torn slivers of what had once been her face hung from the skull like a frill. Her lidless eyes stared, the whites stained red with gore. The muscles of her face twitched as her jaws gnashed in hungry, snarling movements. Wet streaks of fresh blood and leaking body fluid ran from her face like sweat, staining the road beneath.

With Jack in her sights, the woman flipped onto her stomach. She reached forward, her hands grabbing for him. Her long nails were painted with an array of symbols. Red polish atop a black base coat.

She snarled and growled. Her meatless left cheek revealed all of her teeth, extending back into her mouth.

"What the fuck!" Jack yelled, unable to help himself. He crab-walked backwards, stumbling and falling as he went. The woman continued to crawl after him, her speed impressive.

Jack picked up speed in his crab walk, but met opposition in the form of two sets of legs that were standing behind him.

Jack looked back and up in surprise. He saw the two figures, their faces wrapped in the gloomy shroud of a stormy sky.

"Thank fuck. Help us," he cried. "She needs an ambulance, and I—"

His words fell still when a string of intestines spilled from the gut of one of the men. It slapped him in the face as it thrashed from side to side like a snake held against its will.

The man whose insides were dick-slapping his cheek let out a growl. It was an unearthly, guttural raw that eclipsed being a simple cry of pain, confusion, anger and sorrow. It was a sound pulled from the deepest pit of human experience, and melted into the roar of hell beasts. He made the blood in Jack's veins freeze, and for a moment, that was exactly what Jack did.

It was only when the second man dropped to the ground, crushing Jack beneath his weight, pinning him against the concrete, that a will to survive replaced Jack's paralysing fear.

Jack pushed and thrashed and shoved against the man whose throat had been removed. The creature hissed at Jack, over and over. Jack was sure it was trying to produce the same hell-formed growl as his buddy, all that came out was a bubbling rush of hot air.

Blood splattered against Jack's face. It stuck to his eyes, and flooded his mouth. He coughed and choked as the lukewarm crimson fluid coated his mouth and trickled down his throat. It was a heavy, meaty-tasting liquid that made him want to vomit.

The other man had also fallen to the road, his snarls closer to Jack's ear. He felt hands clawing at him, and another clamp down on his foot as the woman finally reached her prize.

"Get off me! Help, help, please," Jack cried out as he continued to fight against those who held him down, seemingly intent on tearing him apart.

Jack kicked out blind and felt the heel of his bare foot connect with the woman. It skipped over her wet face, but the connection was heavy and satisfying enough to push her away.

With his legs free, Jack used them to brace himself, and kicked to his left. He pushed off and forced his way out from under the two brutes. Rolling on the wet tarmac, Jack pushed himself to his feet, but his legs were not ready to take the pressure of supporting his body, and so he fell back to the floor, landing on his ass, staring at the goons who had attacked him.

The two men had clawed their way to their feet and were stumbling towards him again. Their bodies were pale. The blood had stopped flowing from their wounds.

"You … you need help. I can help you," Jack stammered as he once again found himself walking backwards on his hands and feet.

The two gave no response. They just closed the gap on Jack, who turned and tried to get to his feet once again. Rising, he fell into a parked car, grateful for the support it offered him. Hurrying his way around it, he put the car between himself and the two mangled men who were chasing him.

The distance gave him some time to think because the creatures that were once men seemed more interested in moving through the car to get to him, rather than circumventing it in any way.

Jack recognized the man without the throat as the Pakistani man from the shop two streets away. His once friendly and trusting face was contorted by death, his eyes clouded grey like large cataracts.

The second man was a stranger; he was taller than the shop owner, and had a thick beard that was now matted with clumps of dried blood. His lips were pulled back in a snarl, and Jack could see strips of flesh stuck between his teeth. His brain made the immediate association with the faceless woman who was crawling towards the car, seemingly incapable of making it to her feet like her fellow attackers.

"This can't be happening," Jack cried out as his brain began to put all the pieces together. "You're dead."

Jack was not sure if he actually expected any of them to answer, but saying the words was enough to get him moving.

He backed away from the car and looked around. He was on the other side of the street, and saw many faces looking out of their windows. They were watching the world fall to ruin, and too scared to make a move to try to interject.

"Help me," Jack called, but the people he had addressed slid back into the perceived sanctuary of their homes. Safe behind their locked doors and drawn curtains.

Looking around, Jack saw that he was not alone in the streets. There were others, caught unaware, who were suffering the same fate. The earlier mob that had run through his street had not been without casualties. As he watched, a young man in church-worthy attire burst from between the buildings. He stumbled and fell, and two more things descended on him.

They moved with a speed and dexterity that defied their clearly undead status. One was missing an arm, the bloody stump a torn and mutilated lump of flesh. The other was covered in so much gore it was impossible to tell what injury had claimed his life. They sped after the man, who had found his footing once more, and hauled him to the ground.

They tore into his flesh, fingers digging into his chest. Long undead fingers penetrated his body and hooked around his ribs. With a strong tug, they pulled his rib cage apart, and his torso exploded with a wet pop. Blood spurted into the air, showering the two creatures with a shooting cascade of gore.

The man was still alive as the one-armed man buried his head inside the poor soul's gaping chest cavity. There was a wet tearing sound, and the head reappeared with a bloody mouthful of dripping tissue.

Jack could not clearly see what it was, but his imagination filled in the blanks. In any case, it was enough to silence the man's tortured screams, and that in its own right was a blessing.

A growl brought Jack's mind back to his own predicament. The two men had realized that there was a simpler way to get to their prey and were moving around the car. Thinking fast, his strength returned, or at least the surge of adrenaline convinced him that was the case, and Jack leaped at the car. He pushed himself up onto and over the roof in a fluid move. Jack landed on the other side and was met by the persistent, crawling woman. Her raw face looked up and him. Jack hurdled her and found his stride immediately. Running down the street, he bolted back into his building and threw the door shut behind him.

Panicked, he looked around for a way to block it, but then realized it locked automatically and could only be opened from the outside with a key card.

Jack looked at his hand as if for confirmation. At some point in his flight from the living dead, he had pulled the card from his jeans pocket. It was there, clasped in his fingers; covered in blood, much like the rest of him, but it hadn't stopped its effectiveness.

He wondered for a moment if the creatures killed a resident, would they have the wherewithal to be able to use the card to get into the building. He realized soon enough that if that was the case, they were fucked on many more levels than that.

Turning, he bolted up the stairs, his legs turning to jelly as the initial surge of adrenaline wore off. His body shook as he fumbled the key into the lock of his front door.

Jack collapsed the moment he crossed the threshold, falling to the hallway floor. He lay there a while, on his belly, his eyes closed. His world was spinning, his mind unable to process what it had seen now that he had distanced himself from it.

His stomach cramped and he vomited over the floor, chunks of still-to-be-digested pizza crust floated before his eyes on a sea of regurgitated stomach contents.

Crawling through the hall, aware that he was heaving his body through his own vomit but uncaring of the fact, Jack pulled himself to his feet in the living room. He stared out of the window, joining the ranks of the curtain twitchers he had seen in the other building.

The trio were still out there, but had wandered off in their own directions. To the right, the well-dressed man with the expanded chest was alone, his killers long since disappeared, no doubt in search for fresh meat.

The man himself was jerking on the street. His life returned to him in death. He thrashed in wild, jerky movements. Back from the dead and hungry for flesh, yet he appeared to be confined to the location of his demise, unable to right himself without assistance and that would surely never come.

Falling back to the floor, a location he was getting overly familiar with, Jack closed his eyes and tried to block out the foul smell of partially digested undead human offal that was smothered over his face.

"This can't be happening," he spoke aloud. "I've gone crazy. I'm dreaming, that's it. I must be dreaming."

Pulling himself back to his feet, Jack scrambled to find his phone. He needed to get ahold of Sarah. There was still no service. Cursing, he turned back to the television.

The first reports were still continuing with the story about rioters, but as he watched, the images filled the screen. All of them too fleeting to give even the most eagle-eyed viewers more than a second or two to take in the full-scale assault on the nation's capital.

It was only on the third run through the same edited footage that Jack noticed them. Figures within the crowd. Multiple points from which the mass exodus was produced. The riots were a cover. The rising dead were to blame. They were in the city, and from the look of it, in numbers far greater than he could believe.

The pictures came around again, and the final penny dropped. "Motherfuckers!" Jack yelled at the television.

On the fourth image of the riots, still an aerial shot but one made from a closer angle than the others, you could see a building on fire. It was a location that Jack knew well because it was where he had spent many hours of his youth, back when it was an internet café, and also the years after when it became a rather specialist computer supplier.

The problem was, that building had burned to the floor during the 2011 riots. The structure had been saved, but was currently still undergoing renovation. Yet the burning image he saw was clearly still the computer shop.

The realization was a stunning and sobering blow. At some point overnight, while he had been eating pizza and playing video games, the world had gone to hell in a hand basket.

CHAPTER 2

Jack showered and made himself another coffee, desperately trying to convince himself it was all fine. If he went through the usual motions, reality would catch up to him and everything would be fine.

He listened as the screams continued outside. Sometimes there were but one or two, and at other times, it seemed as if the entire borough was yelling as a single pained collective.

One by one, the television channels stopped broadcasting, using excuses pertaining to the riots. It was a rich story as several of the channels were not even broadcasted from London-based studios.

Opening the front door of his flat, Jack looked out. The hallway was a long one with doors along either side. He looked left and right. Somewhere, someone was screaming. Inside their building.

Jack walked out into the hall. Several other doors opened and people appeared. Their eyes were wide with fear, and as soon as Jack turned to look, they shrank away. Mrs. Gloucester from the apartment opposite him actually jumped back inside and slammed the door. Jack heard the double deadbolts slam. Nobody would be getting her out any time soon.

"What's going on?" a voice asked.

Jack turned around and saw a woman, whose name he did not know, standing in an open door. She was holding a young child in her arms.

"I don't know," Jack told her.

"Is it the riots?" she asked, her voice shrouded by a heavy Eastern European accent.

"No, no it's not. It is something else." Jack didn't know what to say to her. "Are you okay, you and your family?"

"It's just us. We are fine," she replied. She was a young woman, not long out of her teens. She looked tired, but it could not hide her pretty features.

Her long auburn hair was pulled back into a rough ponytail, and her make-up free face had a natural beauty to it. She was wearing a white tank top and a pair of black trousers that definitely showed off her shapely legs. She wasn't wearing a bra, a fact that Jack tried hard not to notice.

The child who clung to her was a girl, dressed in a delicate pink dress and a pair of white tights. The child had been crying. Her eyes were red and her cheeks streaked with the stains of her tears.

"Are you sure? You can … you can come to my apartment if you want. I'm alone and, well … I think it is going to get dangerous around here." Jack stared at the woman and hoped she realized he was just as eager to have her over for some company as he believed she was.

"Thank you," she said, stepping out of her flat and into the hall.

A few more doors opened and more people came into the hall. They all shared the same look of fear and confusion.

"Eric," Jack called out when the door to the apartment at the end of the hall opened.

Eric was an acquaintance of Jack's. They knew each other through their choice of lodgings and the fact that neither had a regular job.

The main difference was that while Jack still worked and made more than pretty much anybody he knew, Eric was a stoner. He came from a rich family and spent his days sitting in the weed-infused haze that fogged his flat like a supernatural mist.

"Jack, what's happening, man? I was having a nap and just, fuck, this screaming and shit started. I looked outside and this dude was eating another dude's face. I don't mean like in a gay way but like in a pass-the-bath-salts-I'm-getting-fucking-hungry way. It's all just messed up, man. I don't know what's going on." At some point during his rant, which saw his voice move from a whisper into a scream and back to a whisper, Eric began to cry.

"It's all okay, man. It's just–"

"It's the dead. The dead have risen," a voice called, and an old woman appeared in the hall.

Jack didn't know her name, but he had seen her around. She was well into her eighties, and lived with her son. A single man who had lived at home since the day he was born. Jack had met him once. Queer sort of man, but he certainly left an impression.

"What did she say?" A single voice clarified the sentiment murmured by most of the people milling around on the floor.

"The dead have risen. They crave flesh. Can't you see?" The woman leaned on her walking frame, and took a deep breath. The oxygen tubes that extended from her nose wound around her large frame and connected with the canister that was attached to the wheel-driven walker.

"I don't think–" someone else began to contest, but a scream rang out from the floor above them and everybody was sent scurrying.

The scream was one filled with terror. It lacked the guttural straining of pain, but hit all the right notes for utter, desperate fear.

It brought the nervous chatter to a halt. Everybody froze, and some disappeared back into their flats. Some teamed up, disappearing together into one abode. Safety in numbers and all that.

"What was that?" Eric asked.

"They are inside," the young mother said, her voice trembling.

The child in her arms began to cry.

"No, no they can't be. It's just someone freaking out, or something," Jack tried to reason.

The scream came again, only this time there was a strange finality about the way the voice cut off, just as the pitch reached its zenith.

The way the flats were set up, there were two stairwells that led to each floor and a lift that ran through the centre of the building. There were four floors to the building, but the upper two contained maisonettes, and rather than four flats on each side of the hallway, there were but two.

"We should go check on them," Jack spoke, looking around. Everybody was gone. Only he, Eric, and the young woman were left in the hall.

"Are you crazy?" Eric scoffed, staring at Jack.

"We can't leave her alone up there," Jack shot back.

"She's probably dead," Eric said flatly.

"She's scared," the young mother replied.

Jack and Eric turned to her, both wondering if she meant the woman upstairs, or the daughter in her arms.

"You're right," Jack spoke softly. "You should wait here. Come on, you can stay in my place." He placed his hand on the woman's shoulder and led her through to his apartment.

"Thank you." The woman smiled. "I'm Tania."

"Jack. It's nice to meet you." He smiled, realizing that if what was happening was real, and not some crazy dream, this may be the last formal everyday introduction he shared with someone.

"Thank you for helping us." Tania hugged him. "This is Anna."

The little girl pulled her head from the crook of her mother's neck and smiled at Jack. She had stunning green eyes. They were large orbs on her small face.

"Hi there, heartbreaker." Jack had always been good with children, not that he harboured any desire to have them himself. "You will be safe here. Lock the door behind me."

Jack ran to the kitchen and grabbed a large kitchen knife from the drawer. He said nothing as he moved to the door.

"You're really going to check it out?" Eric looked at him through red-stained eyes.

"Yes, whoever is up there needs help. We can't just ignore that." Jack stood firm. "You can come if you want to help, but if not, make sure that door is locked behind me and doesn't open until I come back."

Eric stood for a few moments, mumbling to himself as he mulled over his options.

"Dammit." He sighed and trudged off into the kitchen.

A few minutes later, the pair emerged from the apartment. The door closed and locked behind them. The atmosphere in the hallway had changed noticeably. Silence dominated the place. A silence that was true to the word. Not the noiseless quiet that most often got confused, but a silence. It was as if people were afraid to even breathe for fear of being found. Even from the streets, there was nothing. Even the rain failed to truly penetrate the spooky ambiance.

"Are you sure about this? It's quiet now." Eric tried once more to get Jack to change his mind, but it was to no avail.

"Come on," Jack replied, determined.

Armed with a kitchen knife and rolling pin, they made their way to the stairs. They could feel the eyes watching them, straining through peepholes to track their progress.

Moving behind one another, weapons raised, they made their way to the third floor. Jack assumed the lead, his heart racing as their every step echoed up the empty chamber.

"You don't really buy all this, do you?" Eric asked. His nerves made him chatty, and the fact that he was high made him all the more paranoid.

"I don't know, man. I'm just taking this one step at a time. If it is true, well, people will be along to save us. I'm sure there are drills and protocols and shit in place for this sort of thing." Jack didn't believe it, but he had to convince himself of something.

They reached the third floor. It was dim, the storm outside having darkened the sky to the colour of dusk. The dark painted walls and the dark floor did nothing to help the matter.

Moving onto the landing, Jack found himself caught in two minds. To call out and risk exposing himself to whatever horror may lurk in the dark, or to stay quiet and hope he happened along whoever was in peril.

Three steps onto the landing and his mind was made up. His foot squelched as he trod. The floor was sodden. Bending down, using his iPhone as a light source, he saw the thick consistency of the red fluid. The closer he got to it, the meatier the taste of the air became.

"What is it?" Eric asked.

"Blood." Jack's answer was met by silence.

"We need to get out of here."

"No, someone could be stuck here," Jack insisted.

His heart was racing and he wanted to be as quiet as possible, but Eric seemed to overcome by his nerves to be quiet.

When they reached the mid-point of the hall, they saw the door at the end was ajar. It was smeared with blood; a streaked handprint ran from the centre to the handle, before falling away to the floor.

Looking at it, Jack could picture the stumbling form that had created it.

He turned to Eric who was still chatting in a low voice, about what, Jack had no clue. Eric had turned to chatting to himself when his conversation with Jack became clearly one sided.

"Keep it quiet, I don't want them to–"

The door behind them crashed open, and a figure came shambling towards them.

The woman's eyes were a dark red as if every vessel behind them had burst. Her lips were pulled back in a snarl. Behind her, more of them appeared, a man and a woman. The woman was wearing a dressing gown, her body beneath clad in a lingerie set stained a rusty shade.

She had a chunk of flesh missing from her shoulder, with deep strips of skin ripped away down to her breast, from where a hungry set of jaws had wrenched her meat from her body.

The pair turned on them. Their steps were stiffened by death but far from the shambling, ambling reanimations of pop culture.

"Get back," Eric cried out, swinging the rolling pin like a rounders bat.

The pair growled at him, a deep and guttural noise. It was demonic in its tone, resonating like a growling death metal singer at the height of live show fervour.

Looking around, Jack backed up. The stairwell at the other end of the hall was their best option. The couple had closed in on them. Eric was still swinging the rolling pin, his feet planted on the floor.

One swing caught the approaching male in the ribs. The sound of the heavy wooden utensil hitting skin was a sickening one, only topped by the audible pop of bone, as ribs snapped from the impact.

The confrontation snapped Eric from his haze, and he turned and ran. The man carried on walking, his body bent to one side ever so slightly, but he showed no long-term effects from the blow.

"Here, through the door," Jack called. He pulled the door open and screamed. A blood-covered corpse turned to face him. The skin was pink and warm, the blood flowed from the wound on the side of the woman's face. Her cheek was missing as was her ear. The bloody bone of her skull visible beneath the mass of matted hair.

Her eyes the same shade of red as the man who was coming for them from the hall.

Jack leaped backwards, letting the door close. It slammed against the dead woman's face, splattering blood, meat, and smears of skin against the wire-glass window.

"Come here," a voice called out.

Jack turned around and saw a face peering through an open door across the hall.

"Hurry," the face implored.

Jack moved, his feet feeling sluggish. He gripped the knife in his right hand. Eric was beside him. They ran towards the room, although to Jack it felt as though they were going in slow motion. The couple was upon them. A hand clamped down on Jack's shoulder. He spun around, survival his only focus. The man's jaws were open, his blood-stained, yellow teeth were closing the distance to Jack's flesh.

Thrusting the knife, Jack stabbed the man in his chest. The knife punctured the skin and sliced deep into the tissue beneath, burying itself to the handle. The man stopped, for a brief moment the knowledge of its injury registered on his face. He shook it off, however, and reached for the fresh meat that he craved. The moment passed. Jack and Eric disappeared into the flat and the door slammed shut.

It was dark in the apartment; the lights were off and all the curtains were drawn. Thick material over roller blinds fully covered the window.

"Thank you," Jack spoke to the hazy figure of their rescuer. He was out of breath, and his hand was slick with blood from where he had stabbed the man in the hallway.

"I'm sorry," the voice whimpered.

"Sorry for what?" Jack asked as a shudder ran through him.

"I couldn't leave you to die out there, but …" The voice trailed off and was replaced by a hungry growl.

Eric gave a cry, and in the darkness, all hell broke loose. The woman who had saved them started to cry. Uttering her apologies over and over again as she pushed Jack out of the way. He was off balance and disoriented by the darkness. He pitched forward, stretching his arms out to brace himself.

The door to the room opened, and he saw a figure slip out into the hall.

Jack careened into the wall, cracking his knee against a small table. Pain erupted in his leg; a sharp stabbing sensation that travelled through his lower leg and into his foot. Buckling, his leg not capable of supporting him, Jack stumbled sideways. As he fell, his hand raked down the wall, and caught the light switch.

Brightness filled the room, and he was just in time to see a very large elderly woman flatten Eric. She was easily three hundred pounds, her sagging skin blooming from her body in thick, doughy rolls. The front of her hospital nightgown was covered in a mixture of blood and a thick, yellow substance the consistency of oatmeal. It stunk of regurgitation, which fit with the stale, airless aroma that hung in the abode.

Eric was pinned beneath the woman, whose slobbering jowls were snapping furiously, her weight driving her closer and closer to his neck.

Thinking fast, Jack struck out, kicking the fat woman in the ribs. It felt like kicking concrete. His already-aching leg rang out in pain again as the jolt of the flesh-on-flesh impact reverberated through his body. Raising his foot, he kicked out again, only this time pushing with his heel. He kicked against the side of the woman's head. Her skull whipped to the right as a result of the impact, but was soon snapping and snarling once more.

Jack raised his foot and kicked again and again, driving his heel into the side of the woman's head. A rage built in him. A rage driven by fear and adrenaline mixing inside his brain, marinating it in a violent sauce and forcing him lose control.

He screamed and cried out as the obese neck gave an audible snap and twisted to one side. The woman wasn't dead, far from it, but her teeth were at least aimed away from Eric's neck.

Working together, the two men rolled the large frame over to one side. They failed to fully rotate the woman, but they created enough room for Eric to worm his way out from beneath her.

The woman fell back onto her face, her deformed neck bulging in all the wrong places. She growled and rocked, her enormous belly creating a see-saw effect as a result of her hunger-driven thrashings. She rocked back and forth as long, thin hair whipped around her, her nightgown riding higher and higher, exposing the undulating fleshy mounds of her upper thighs and buttocks, which were covered in veins and weeping sores.

"Are you alright?" Jack asked, his chest tight, his lungs burning.

"Yeah ... yeah, I think so," Eric said, looking at Jack with a clarity in his eyes that he had never seen before.

It turned out that the zombie apocalypse was enough to snap a stoner out of a multi-year long high.

"Let's get out of here," Jack suggested.

"How? We can't go out there. Those ... those things." Eric was struggling, his body was shaking and his eyes were nervously surveying everything in sight for fear of attack.

"We don't have a choice." Jack looked at him. "There are only two of them. That woman, whoever she was, she ran out there, she must have thought she had a chance. I say we grab something to arm ourselves with, and run for it. We make it to the stairs, we get the others to block them off."

The plan was made before Jack knew he was talking. They searched the two-floored apartment for signs of weaponry. The second floor was as good as empty, save for storage. The obese woman had condensed her life down to two rooms. The multi-purpose cross-functioning living room, and the kitchen.

There was little in terms of decoration on the walls; no pictures of loved ones, children, or grandchildren. The oxygen tank and medical equipment around the bed were interesting, but not much use when fighting off the undead.

As it was, they armed themselves in a similar fashion to when they set off, Eric grabbing a large carving knife, and a serrated-edged bread knife, while Jack took hold of a heavy iron skillet pan – an old-fashioned pan. He hoped it would hold up and deliver and old-fashioned thrashing as a result.

"What's that?" Jack pointed at the blood trickling over Eric's hand.

"Nothing. Bitch's nails scratched me, that's all. I'm good, I promise." Eric sensed the apprehension in Jack's voice and saw his nervous stare.

They opened the door to the hallway and ran out. The initial attack they had both feared was gone. The zombie from the stairwell was still trapped behind the door, her mangled face was pressed hard against the glass, as if she were trying to pass through it.

The two undead monsters were oblivious to their initial emergence for they were both preoccupied, feasting on the torn-open remains on the woman who had lured Jack and Eric into the apartment.

She was wearing what remained of a nurse's uniform, and, Jack doubted it was because the fat woman was kinky.

The woman had made it half way to her escape, but now she lay on her back, her legs spread and her guts pulled apart. Thick strands of organs and meat lay scattered about where the undead had descended on her in a frenzy, not caring what was discarded as long as there was more remaining to be shovelled into their hungry mouths.

"Just run," Jack said when he saw Eric freeze behind him.

The head of the female creature whipped up, and her grey eyes locked on Jack. She rose from the floor, a string of raw meat dangling from her lips. She sucked it up like a strand of spaghetti, and advanced on them.

Jack and Eric broke into a run, swiping out as they did. The male turned and blocked their path, inadvertent as it was. Jack wasted no time. He raised the skillet like a battle axe, and roared as he swung it down in a near vertical arc. The heavy pan connected with the dead man's skull in a heavy, meaty thwack.

The bone was crushed like an empty soda can. Blood spurted from his ears, nose, and mouth, while his eyeballs bulged and grey brain fluid leaked from behind them. The weight of the pan carried on and out of Jack's hands, falling to the floor, leaving the man with half a head. The scalp split open and jagged shards of shattered skull lined the long gash. It looked, to Jack at least, like a cracked egg, broken open, emptied, and discarded.

The man fell to the floor, and what remained of his brain leaked out to merge with the ever-deepening pool of blood.

Hurdling him, leaving the woman behind, Jack and Eric made it to the stairs. They jumped from one floor to another, sliding with blood and sweat-slicked hands down the railings.

"Help, help, everybody. We need to block the doors," Jack shrieked the moment they barrelled through the stairwell door back on the second floor. "Quick, somebody, we need to block the doors."

Whether it was the community spirit coming back to the crowd, the intensity behind Jack's wild shrieks, or a selfish sense of survival rising in each individual, Jack didn't know. All he saw was that the doors opened and people came out to see what was going on.

Within minutes, people were pushing and pulling all manner of furniture and belongings to block the doors at the end of the hallway.

"No, not that one, otherwise we are stuck here," Jack called out when he saw a similar tactic being employed to the door at the other end.

"We need to do something," a scared voice snapped back.

"Block the stairs themselves. Fill them up, but we need to keep a way out." Jack was not sure why he was suddenly the man people were looking to for orders, but he answered their questions, and couldn't help but watch as people began to listen.

It didn't take long before everybody had sealed the upper floor from the lower. Those that had helped were drenched in sweat and just as scared as ever. Jack saw the young woman standing in his doorway, the child now missing from her arms. She looked at Jack and smiled. He found himself returning the gesture, and being genuinely pleased at seeing her again. The fact that he could have died just by going to look at the third floor of his own apartment building had not filtered through his overloaded mind until that moment.

"Are there still people up there?" she asked as Jack crossed the hall towards her.

"I hope not," he answered. A shudder ran through him as he realized another component of his poorly thought out plan. "If there are, I just sentenced them to death."

"You did what needed to be done," a strong voice answered.

Jack turned around and saw a man he recognized, but could not name. The building was, for the most part, a friendly one, but not close. It was not the suburbs; people did not get together for drinks and barbeques in the summer. For the most part, people kept to themselves. They said hello and enjoyed the causal relationship of acquaintances, but not much more than that.

Jack didn't answer the man, but nodded his appreciation.

With their floor secure, everybody disappeared back into their respective caves, eager to surround themselves with what they knew, and hoped it would be enough to block out the echoing growls that seemed to travel through the building like a whispering call of madness.

CHAPTER 3

Jack locked the door to his apartment, and turned to face the two people who stood there.

Tania was staring at him with her large hazel eyes. Her thanks, her fear, everything she felt was wrapped in the silent communication that passed between them.

Eric stood beside her, his body crusted in blood and the dried smear of yellow vomit.

Jack didn't know what to say. Words failed him. Not because he could not think of anything that was either witty or comforting, but because his brain had literally failed him. He could not utter a single word.

"That was intense." Eric broke the silence as he scratched at his blood-encrusted skin. Thick flakes of rusted blood fell to the floor.

"Uh-huh," Jack stuttered, feeling proud that he managed to string such a comprehensive response together.

Jack walked away from the door and into his living room. He collapsed onto the sofa, without saying a word. Tania collapsed next to him. They looked at each other, staring at one another, lost in a trance as everything was being processed.

"I'm going to take a shower. Can I use yours?" Eric asked, seemingly adjusted to the change in the world.

"Sure," Jack offered, once again impressed at his own linguistic skills.

Eric wandered away, and a few moments later, they heard the water of the shower running.

"Are you okay?" Jack asked Tania

"Yes, are you?" she asked, likewise stoic in her body language and emotional involvement in the conversation.

Jack stared at their reflections in the television screen. They looked like a married couple, together, side by side, running through their day, not because of any real concern or interest, but because it was part of the deal. It was a package affair and such questions belonged there.

"Where is Anna?" Jack turned to look at her now.

"She is sleeping. I hope that is okay." The questioning tone of her voice made her sound worried.

"Of course. She can sleep as long as she needs. I know I won't be sleeping ever again." Jack tried to laugh at his joke, but then he realized he was most likely telling the truth.

"What was up there?" Tania asked. "We could hear, something, banging and screaming, and we thought you were dead, too." Her voice fell away to a whisper.

"Do you really want to know?" Jack could sense her fear, and had the feeling that it went beyond what had happened that day.

"I need to. I need to know so I can protect my daughter." Tania's voice gained strength when she spoke of her daughter.

"She's beautiful," Jack told her, hoping to reassure her. "She takes it from her mother." He paused, regretting he had said it. "I'm sorry, that sounds very bad, I don't mean it like that, I just mean—"

Tania started to laugh, not even a laugh, it was a giggle, a light and refreshing sound. "I understand, and thank you."

"It was bad up there." Jack sat back, forcing himself to talk about what he had seen. It was real, it was all real, and they had to accept it or die. "There were people up there; they were dead. They were dead, but alive. Undead, zombies, creatures, call them anything you want, but they are up there. They came for us, and, well, there was someone else there, too. She was alive, but they got her. They ripped her open and ate her alive." Jack ran through the events, sparing the detailed descriptions. There was no need to share that burden.

"What will we do?" Tania asked, tears brimming in her eyes.

"Wait, I guess. I mean, I've seen movies, read books. There are always evacuations. Military, at least early on. They will tell us what we need to do. We have enough food here, and we are safe enough." Jack ran through his plan. It was not a masterful attempt at survival strategy. It was not brave, but it was the most he could do.

As the day wore on, the sound of sirens reached a fervour and then died down. The news reports that were still broadcasted held up the pretence of the riots before they too went off the air.

The streets were quiet. Nobody dared to venture outside. Eric had his shower and emerged clean, but in the same blood-soaked clothing he had been wearing before.

When it was clear that he had no interest in leaving the group, even if to just go across the hall to his own apartment for clothing, Jack offered him some clean clothes. He chose a ridiculous outfit of long white shorts and a bright red and yellow shirt. They were actually Terry's from a party he had been to the previous summer.

Eric said nothing as he pulled on the clothes, rescuing a fat joint from his gore-encrusted trouser pocket.

"Do you mind?" he asked, lighting up before anybody had the chance to answer.

Jack spent most of the afternoon sitting by the window, watching the world. The rain continued in some form or another, the sky changing from black to varying shades of grey, before moving back to thunderous darkness again.

Every now and then, somebody would be seen running across the street. As afternoon arrived and the silence became deafening, the first groups of people made their move. They emerged with bags and suitcases. Filling cars in short-sprinted bursts. Families piled inside, looking like clowns at the circus. It amazed Jack just how much it seemed, could be squeezed inside a small hatchback, it just depended on the level of motivation.

All along, the reanimated corpse of the church-going man with a hollowed-out chest cavity lay there, his arms reaching furiously every time it heard a noise. Jack was pretty sure that if he opened the window, he would hear it growling.

He didn't, however, because he was terrified of what else he might hear.

"She's hungry," Tania spoke. She had been sitting close to Jack ever since they had sealed themselves in the single floor home. When he moved to the sofa, she followed, when he moved to the window, she followed.

They spoke very little, but the comfort that was both offered and found simply by being close to someone else was powerful.

"I have some food. What does she like?" Jack replied, getting to his feet and heading towards the kitchen.

"Bread is good. A sandwich, or soup," Tania said, following close behind Jack, Anna in her arms, her face buried in her mother's neck.

Above them, something heavy banged on the floor. It made everybody in the flat jump.

"What do you think caused it?" Tania asked as Jack handed her the sandwich he had made.

"I figured she didn't eat the crusts. I never did when I was a kid," he said as he looked at the plate.

"Thank you," Tania answered, sitting down on the sofa, placing Anna beside her. Almost instantly, the little girl grabbed at the small triangular sandwiches.

"I don't know what could have caused it," Jack finally answered. "In the movies, it is always the flu, or something like that, but this … there was nothing like that. Last night, everything was normal, and today, well, today it is all just crazy."

Beside them, curled up in the chair, Eric slept. In spite of his initial exuberance, it had worn off and left him a lot more withdrawn than either of them would have expected.

"It had to be something. People changed. The dead, should stay dead." Tania looked at her daughter as she spoke, and stroked her hair behind her ears.

"Well, whatever happens, you guys are safe here with me. You can stay as long as you need. Until they come for us." Jack smiled and sat back in his chair.

Pulling his phone out of his pocket, he tried to call Sarah, but there was still no service. He could not hide his worry, and he dropped the phone into his lap.

"Who are you calling?"

"My girlfriend. She is in the city with her mother."

"I'm sorry." Tania looked at him.

"Thank you. I'm sure she is fine. This just needs to be contained, that's all." Jack knew it was a lie, but it was one he had to believe.

As evening hit, more people appeared in the street. Clearly hoping that the cover of darkness would help aid their escape. Jack watched as a man stumbled towards a couple who were trying to unlock their car door. He wanted to call out, to warn them about the shambling figure that was bearing down on them.

He didn't. As his fists were about to pound the glass, he thought about how doing so would draw attention. It would show them, the undead, that people were alive up there.

As it happened, the figure walked by the couple, stopping only after he had passed to take a long drink from an indistinguishable bottle.

"They are leaving," Tania said, joining Jack by the window.

"They are scared," he replied.

"So am I." She looked at Jack.

"Do you live alone?" Even though he'd asked her this before, Jack wanted to take his mind off the situation outside.

"Yes. My family is all in Poland."

"Poland, that's interesting. What brought you out here?" Jack asked, genuinely interested.

"The lifestyle. I always loved to look at England. At English girls. I wanted to have that, to be that. So I saved my money, my wages from my job, and when I had enough, I left Poland and came here. Four years ago, when I was seventeen."

"What about Anna's father?" Jack had never seen anybody coming and going in Tania's flat, but he was not one to sit and watch everybody that closely.

"He died before he knew about Anna. A car crash." There was sadness in Tania's voice, but her face remained strong.

"I'm sorry." Jack felt like an ass for asking. "It's getting dark."

"Yes, I think I'm going to sleep. She is tired, but she won't sleep alone."

Jack got up from the table, and took the empty coffee cups through to the kitchen.

"You can stay in my room. I will sleep in the spare room." Jack pointed to the room that was his.

"Thank you, Jack. You are a good man." She gave him a hug and picked Anna from the sofa. "We will see you in the morning. Tomorrow, we will need to make some decisions." She did not wait for further discussion but slipped into the room and closed the door.

Eric was still passed out on the chair. He was breathing lightly, but had not moved in a long time. Jack debated on waking him but realized he didn't really want to spend the evening chatting. He liked the silence. Making himself a cocoa, a tradition since his childhood, he sat back down by the window and drank until he felt drowsy.

Outside, a large group of people moved through the street. They were singing and laughing. Jack couldn't help but wonder if it was because they didn't know the truth. He thought, sadly enough, that it was most likely that they just chose to ignore it. They were all men, and they had been drinking, that much was clear. They were putting on some macho display, proving they were not afraid of the undead.

Jack had not contemplated sleep. He had naturally assumed that after everything he had seen that day, sleep would be the last thing his brain would allow. He was wrong. Sliding into Terry's bed, he was asleep not long after he closed his eyes.

Dreams came, and while they were not pleasant, they were not the horror-filled nightmares that Jack had expected. There were no undead creatures walking around, flesh dribbling from their mouths. Instead, he was lost in a fog. A thick haze that smothered everything. Someone was holding his hand. Their fingers interlocked in his own. He looked but could not see who it was. He felt alone, and as he walked, an endless march through a never-changing field of grey, he kept squeezing the hand that held his own. Even though he could not see the owner, he kept going, because they gave him the strength to do so.

CHAPTER 4

The scream snatched Jack from his dreams, and yanked him viciously into the cold, harsh reality of the early morning.

He jumped from the bed, lost and confused. It was not his room. The scream came again, a two-level shriek. No, two cries. Two very different cries.

Jack ran. He crashed into the desk chair in the middle of the room. The pain rang out from his second toe. Jack swallowed the string of curses he wanted to scream. The injury had the beneficial effect of blowing away the cobwebs of sleep from his mind.

He burst from the room, charging into the living room he recognized. He looked around. There was nobody. The scream came again. It came from inside his room.

Jack swallowed hard as he remembered Tania and her daughter. He had let them stay in his room because of the undead.

The undead. They were real.

Jack hurdled the sofa and charged into the room. He was armed with an antique paperweight. The large, round glass structure was solid and had the potential in it to deal out decimating blows.

Jack took one look around his room, and wished he had not done so.

The table lamp was on, and cast a dim glow that lit up just enough of the room for the gruesome scene to be witnessed in full Technicolour.

Eric was standing by the bed, backing Tania, who was screaming, and Anna into the corner. Eric was growling, and Jack could see the subtle grey hue of his skin.

"Eric," he called, but the figure did not react.

In a frantic burst of movement, Eric lunged for the terrified pair, a guttural noise that exceeded far beyond a mere growl. Likewise, Jack lunged forward, grabbing at the form that had once been Eric.

Eric turned his upper body and swung an arm. The dead weight of his flesh resulted in a powerful backhanded blow that caught Jack across the side of his jaw. Jack veered from his intended course and crashed over the bed and into the wall.

Tania, to her credit, tried to take advantage of the distraction. She burst into a run, determined to sprint her way to freedom. Undead Eric was too quick for them, however. His snarling face snapped towards their movement, and his burning red eyes darkened as he struck.

Teeth sank into soft and tender flesh, a sudden jerk of the neck sufficient to shear a large chunk of blood-dripping meat out of Anna's side.

The child gave a cry that ran into an ear-piercing wail. She thrashed in her mother's arms, sending thick spurts of young blood into the air.

Eric chewed and swallowed the meat, smiling as he moved in for seconds.

He didn't get that chance. The heavy paperweight smashed into his skull, splitting the skin at the first attempt and splattering the walls with blood with the second and all subsequent strikes. Jack roared as he tapped into a deep-seated fury. He swung and swung until his arms ached. Each clubbing blow gouging out more and more chunks of flesh, bone, and brain. By the time Jack dropped the trophy, a memento of his academic prowess in school, it was a battered and twisted reminder of his first step towards acceptance of the undead, and the ushering in of a new world. Eric's body lay on the floor, twitching as the final remnants of his second life leeched into the old carpet along with his pulverized brain.

Panting and covered in blood, Jack looked up and saw Tania running through the living room towards the front door.

Pushing aside the stomach-churning nausea that came as a result of what he had done, Jack gave chase.

"Tania, wait," he cried out as she yanked the door open and sped into the hall. Jack was not far behind her, his determined stride had him moving faster than her panicked flight.

With her bleeding, screaming child clasped tight in her arms, Tania sped through the hallway. Her screams had given way to a silent determination. She needed to escape. She disappeared into the dark stairwell and took the steps two or three at a time, her footing even though her stride was ungainly.

"Wait, it's not safe." Jack watched Tania disappear into the stairwell, and without thinking, ran after her.

The hallway was dark, the lighting dim at best during the early morning hours, a strange quirk of the housing association, who thought it rather unsightly to have hall lights on full power when people were trying to sleep. Still, even the dim light was enough to stop Jack in his tracks.

The barricade that had been erected was holding firm, however, it did not fully block off the stairs. Eager to succeed, the woman who had met her death on the floor above, sought to share her second chance at life with those below. She had climbed onto the pile of furniture and belongings, pulling herself over them, inching her way towards the end.

Only, her death had resulted in a large gash being opened across her belly region, and while all of the blood had been shed before she expired, the jutting legs of crudely piled tables and chairs had been sufficient to hook themselves into her open wound and further tear her flesh. A string of intestines extended behind her almost the length of the stairwell blockade.

The organs had been torn and ruptured, and the stench of fermenting faeces and the early onset of rot in the slimy innards was overpowering. The undead woman saw Jack, and her energy was renewed. She pulled herself with a vigour that saw her flesh rip around her back and over her spine. Her flesh peeled away, exposing bone and muscle below. None of that seemed to matter, though. Not when there was fresh meat for the taking.

Beneath him, Jack heard the doors to the ground floor close, and he found control again. He turned, and for the second time in less than twenty-four hours, he was racing down the stairs. Only now, he was closer to leaping them in a single stride, landing hard each time, using the wall to stop his forward momentum and to push off his next stage of descent.

Outside, the morning was cool, the scent of the rain from the previous day heavy in the air. Even in the pre-dawn murk, it was easy to tell that the forecast for the coming day would be very similar.

Being as early as it was, Jack had been prepared for the quiet. It was to be expected. What he had not expected was the constant, but distant groan. It was a subtle sound that carried on the air. It was a chilling noise because Jack knew what creatures created such a lifeless groan. He also understood that for the noise to permeate through the air to such an extent, there were more than just a handful of the creatures roaming the streets.

Looking around, Jack saw Tania bolting between the buildings on the other side of the street. He gave chase without thinking.

He ran, his legs driving against the wet floor, his lungs burning from the exertion thus far. Sweat slicked his body, and the general damp in the air was drenching him also. He wanted to call out but understood what a bad idea that might be. So he followed, and with every stride, he gained some ground, closing the distance between them. With every stride, the silence, the lack of screaming, weighed heavier on it.

Jack finally caught up with Tania in the park. She had collapsed by a tree, shrouded by darkness. Had it not been for her deep, heart-breaking sobs, Jack would have struggled to see her.

"Tania," he began, walking towards her.

She sat on the ground, her back against the tree. She was caked in blood, and clutching Anna in her arms.

She raised her head to look at Jack as he approached, but she was unable to speak. Grief overpowered her. She looked down at her child, and back at Jack, her mouth open, strands of spit tracing from her upper to lower lip and back again, as if her mouth had been sewn shut and now tore open in order to give voice to her emotion.

Jack stopped close. He didn't want to look, yet, at the same time, he could not stop his eyes from absorbing the scene. Anna looked like a doll in her mother's arms, a pale, blood-covered doll.

"My baby," she wept, the first words she had spoken since it had happened.

Jack tried to think how long ago it had been. It felt like hours, a lifetime even. Every second that passed surrounded by the presence of such young tragedy felt like a lifetime stripped away from his soul. In reality, it could not have been more than a few minutes.

"It's not safe out here." Jack didn't realize how redundant that statement was until it was too late.

"It's not safe anywhere," Tania shrieked, rising to her feet, clutching Anna to her, kissing her head over and over, as if she could somehow replace the missing lump of flesh and breathe fresh life back into her daughter.

The blood came from nowhere, or so it seemed. One minute Tania was crying and kissing her child, and the next, a torrent of dark red blood spewed from her mouth, covering both herself and Anna.

Tania's eyes widened, and she moved to stare at Jack. Her body went limp, and Anna tumbled from her arms, falling to the ground with a heavy thud. Tania followed soon after, landing face first on top of her daughter. The back of her neck was missing, the vertebrae exposed in the ever-increasing light of a new day.

The dead hobo who was savagely chewing the lump of prime flesh he had stolen emerged from the dark. His long, hard, and thick chest-length beard was sticky with blood, and as Jack looked, he saw a severed finger hanging from the man's tangled facial locks.

He staggered forward, his body bloated, coated from head to toe in grime and dirt. A foul stench emanated from his body, and Jack was sure that he would have smelled as bad in life, also.

Unarmed and unsure of everything around him, Jack was in no position to fight back. He backed up, his eyes not locked on the zombie, but on the two tangled bodies that lay on the floor.

Turning to run, Jack saw three more creatures stumbling in the street. They looked like they belonged to the party of men he had seen earlier in the night. Clearly, their bravado got the better of them.

Ducking to his right, Jack tried to turn back into the park, hoping to use the shadows to escape the undead hobo and at least buy himself some time. The hobo was caught unaware, and even gave a confused growl when he realized his second course had evaded him.

The problem was that there were half a dozen other flesh-munching, reanimated corpses meandering their way through the park. Each of them were covered in gore. One had been gutted completely, the flesh ripped away from his rib cage, exposing the protective casing to the world. Another had a large chunk missing from his thigh, and subsequently walked with a limp that under any other circumstance would have been insanely comical.

The others were so covered in blood it was impossible to tell what blood came from them and what came from their victims.

Jack was trapped. He looked around, and felt surrounded. The undead were acting alone, converging on fresh meat, but it was as good a trap as many could have created.

There were gaps between them all, and with each shuffled metre gained on him, those gaps closed.

Residential properties surrounded the park on all sides. To the west was a train station, which would connect him straight to the city. Not that he expected many trains to be running. To the east was a pub. It was one that he had frequented regularly over the years he had been living in the apartment.

Jack didn't know why those places came to his mind at that particular moment, but neither were of any use.

Jack ran forward, deep into the park. He had no idea where he was going to go, but he soon had an idea, one that might have just saved his life.

The bandstand was a feature of the park. It was never used for anything resembling its real purpose. The inside was covered with graffiti and was a popular spot for drunken couples to come and fuck under the watchful eye of the night. Surprisingly, it was unoccupied when Jack arrived, not that it mattered, for he was not looking to find shelter in the structure, but rather, on it. Jumping up, Jack managed to grab the overhanging roof and haul himself up and onto the gently slanting surface.

Rolling onto his back, keeping himself as flat as possible, Jack closed his eyes. He closed his eyes in the hope that he was dreaming. He wanted to shut out everything, to give his mind a chance to focus.

Jack jolted, his eyes springing open, and his abs contracting to pull him upright. It took a moment before he realized what was happening. It was his phone. It was vibrating.

CHAPTER 5

Frantic and uncoordinated, Jack fumbled to try to pull his phone free. Ultimately, it popped from his pocket and slid through his clumsy fingers. It skidded down the roof of the bandstand, eliciting a cry of despair from Jack.

He lunged forward and grabbed the phone just as it began to disappear over the edge. He pulled back quickly when an undead arm snatched at his hand. He looked down to see Tania staring at him. Her eyes were a cloudy grey, although behind the cloud, he could still make out a faint trace of the rich hazel colour that had been such a striking sight. Her blood-soaked body was twisted as she reached up for him. Her mouth pulled back into a snarl. Her skin had already started to pale, a sullen grey hue.

For a moment, Jack was lost to the horror and forgot about his phone. Clawing his way back up to the centre of the hexagonal roof, Jack swiped his thumb over the screen.

"Hello?" he called, almost yelling into the device.

For a heart-stopping moment, Jack thought he was too late. He had blown it. He heard nothing but static.

"Jack?" The voice was distant and crackled, like the recordings of old police interviews or 999 calls. Yet Jack would have recognized the voice even if it had been nothing but a single syllable that had made it through the bad connection.

"Sarah?" Jack couldn't believe it.

The wave of relief that washed over him was immeasurable. It was like waking up late, having slept through the alarm only to realize it was Saturday, and then magnified a hundred times.

"Jack, something's happened …"Sarah's voice crackled before falling away again.

"I know, I know. The dead rose. Not exactly what you call a normal weekend. This is why you should not leave me to my own devices," Jack joked. His body shook as part of the weight on him sprang free and drifted off into the great unknown.

"I thought you would just sit around eating pizza and playing video games," Sarah said, finishing with a laugh.

"Where are you?" Jack realized he did not know how long the signal would last, and had better make some practical use of it.

"We are in the theatre. Those things, they came during the show. The police and military are everywhere, Jack. We can't leave." The fear that she had hidden until that point, rose with a flourish in those three small words.

"Why not? The army is there. They will help, surely. Just hold tight," Jack spoke, faltering only when he heard Sarah's sobs.

"You don't understand, Jack. They are killing people."

"The undead?"

"No, the army, the police. They are killing anybody they see. London is gone. There are so many of those things." The voice fell away and silence took over the line. "Run, Jack." Sarah's voice came back just long enough to say the words, before the connection was lost.

"Sarah … Sarah," Jack called into the phone over and over. It was no use. The signal was lost.

Jack shot to his feet on the bandstand roof, holding his phone aloft, as if it could somehow reconnect if he held it a few feet higher than normal.

Sarah was alive, and that was all Jack needed to know. Everything that had happened in the previous twenty-four hours was done, and nothing could bring anybody back. Eric, Tania, even little Anna. They were gone and lost forever. Jack knew what he had to do.

The undead Tania was still snarling at the roof of the bandstand, and while some other creatures were starting to wander in his general direction, they were still far enough away to give Jack a chance.

He sprang from the roof and landed hard. He remembered to tuck his shoulder and roll. His plan to spring straight to his feet and start running failed, and he just ended up in a heap on the floor.

Running through the park, Jack built his plan as he went. He needed to get into London. He didn't know how or what he expected to do. If the military had lost control and were just shooting at anybody who moved, then there were bigger problems afoot than just the undead.

Still that was a problem for another time. First, he needed to get a car.

Jack had a license, although he had not driven in several years or had never actually owned a car. Still, he thought it unlikely he would get stopped and done for not having insurance with everything else that was going wrong. A parking ticket, sure; those cunts would work through a nuclear holocaust if it meant hitting their quota of fines.

The park was deeper than Jack remembered, and his pace had slowed to a jog before he exited on the far side, his lungs burning and his legs heavy as lead.

The number of undead were increasing at an alarming rate, and while Jack had already noticed that there seemed to be different sorts of them, every one he had seen thus far in the park were far more the movie stereotype. Only Tania was different. There was something behind her eyes. Not so much a part of her that resisted, but a part of her that was still who she had been.

A larger man, with a sagging beer gut, lurched out from behind a tree. He was missing an eye, the right-hand side of his face a messy pulp of minced flesh. He growled and swung an angry, clubbing blow, but Jack altered his course and sped by.

The street on the far side of the park was not dissimilar to his own, except the properties were large family homes rather than flats. Each one three full floors of high ceilings, glorious history, and expensive, almost unaffordable upkeep.

There were a few people outside. Including a family who were trying hard to shepherd everybody out of their house and into the waiting minivan. The driver's door was open and the engine was running. The car itself fully stocked with clothes and supplies.

The family of four were hurrying down the steps. The father and eldest child were first, carrying one final suitcase between them. After them came the mother and daughter. Both were crying, the daughter uncontrollably so. She clung to her mother as if she would be lost if her grip was somehow broken.

For a moment, Jack thought about stealing the car. Just jumping behind the wheel and leaving them behind. He chided himself as soon as the thought arose.

The undead forced his hand somewhat, however, for once the father's throat had been ripped out by the blood-covered, reanimated corpse that seemed to appear through the darkness, the rest of the family's fate was sealed.

The mother stopped in her tracks. She turned to sprint upstairs but lost her footing and fell. She pitched forward, and the sound of her head bouncing from the edge of the concrete steps was something that seemed to roll heavy on the air. What was the worst, as far as Jack was concerned, was the silence. The son and the mother made no sound at all. The mother not as she fell, her neck snapping backwards as she bounced her way down the steps, her terrified daughter trapped beneath her, still unwilling to break her hold. The boy was silent as the second creature reached him, its claw-like fingers raking deep gouges of flesh from the side of his face. Blood pulsed in thick spurts. It looked black.

The scent of blood and meat wafted on the early morning breeze, and combined with the heavy, storm-filled atmosphere, it made Jack want to vomit.

Jack knew he should move to help the family, but only the little girl was left, and a crowd of three undead monsters had already descended. They tore their way through the mother, and would simply keep on digging until they got her, too.

Jack ran for the car, opening the passenger door. He jumped across the seat and slid behind the wheel.

His movements caught the attention of one creature who turned and glared. It had a mouthful of meat dribbling from its lips, long strands of torn muscle dangling like spaghetti. The creature reached out and grabbed hold of Jack.

Jack saw it coming and moved just enough to ensure the dead man's grip closed around the seatbelt buckle.

Not waiting any longer, Jack threw his foot onto the gas pedal. The car lurched forward. Thankfully, it was an automatic, because Jack forgot all about gears and the concept of shifting through them.

The minivan surged forward, its engine groaning from the savage gunning it was being given. The car sped down the road with the undead man still holding on. It was growling and roaring as its legs dragged along the tarmac, stripping away layer after layer of dead tissue and flesh. The creature seemed not to notice, and heaved itself closer to the open driver's side door.

Jack accelerated a little more and then slammed on the brakes. Not only was the hungry corpse unable to stop its momentum in such a speedy fashion, but it collided head first with the door that was whipped closed by the sudden stop.

The skull burst, caving in on the far side. Dark, clotted blood streaked the door that bounced open.

Reaching out, Jack grabbed the door and pulled it closed. Again and again he slammed it shut. The creature's head was crushed further and further before it was fully separated from the rest of the body. Even after decapitation the arm held fast, its grip on the belt unyielding.

Jack slammed the door again and the arm broke, the bones crunching from the impact. The skin tore like that of a piece of overripe fruit. The fingers were still locked, but with the head and now the body gone, Jack felt safe to act. Grabbing the severed limb in his hand, flinching at the cold touch of the flesh, he yanked and tore it loose. He threw it to the floor and gunned the gas once more just as the two remaining creatures stumbled to the back of the car.

They stood in the background as Jack drove away. They did not give chase, but simply turned around and wandered away, each going their own separate direction.

Jack tried to focus on the road, but his heart was racing. He was slick with sweat, and his vision kept blurring as wave after wave of nauseating stomach cramps washed over him.

Jack turned his head to the side as a thick expulsion of green vomit surged from his gut. It shot from his throat like a hurled projectile, splattering the passenger-side window. The first burst missed the seat completely, but the second took care of it, making up for the first attempt by soaking the fabric with thick, sour-smelling disgorge.

Ignoring the growing stench in the car, Jack focused on the road, and avoiding the ever-growing crowd of the undead who seemed increasingly interested in his minivan. His car of choice was admittedly a poor one.

It was at least fourteen years old, and made more noise than an old Skoda trying to start on a cold morning. However, it was all he had, and as long as it kept him moving towards the city and Sarah, Jack did not care.

The ride didn't last long. While the shaking, rattling, but somehow still-rolling beast managed to draw the attention of the roaming undead, it also had the added bonus of warranting longing glances from the living.

Not fifteen minutes after his journey began, Jack was forced to test the car's brakes. He was travelling at around sixty, not caring much for the sad, red, electronic faces that were trying to guilt him into slowing his speed.

The kid appeared from nowhere. He said kid, but in reality they were in their mid-teens, and closer to his age than he would want to admit. The girl, who had the look of one significantly older, and above the age of consent that she surely was, stood in the middle of the road. Her rather large, early developed breasts were sheathed by a red lace bra. Her lower half was dressed in a matching pair of red lace hipster briefs. Her ribs were coloured with bruises, and even in the dim light of morning and the glaring light of the car's headlights, Jack could see the outline of the fist that had delivered many of the blows.

"Stop," she called, her hands raised above her head.

His heart had leaped into his throat where it continued to pound like a son of a bitch.

Jack opened the car door, his first instinct being to bring the girl inside the car and get to safety. The second instinct, the one that came too late, was to duck.

The fist came from out of nowhere, or so it seemed. As large as a saucepan, it smacked against the side of Jack's head and turned out his lights. By the time he hit the road, he was vaguely aware of where he was, but it was already too late.

The girl screamed as the large man grabbed her by the hair and threw her into the car.

"We can't leave him," she protested, but a savage backhand across her face shut her up. She fell into the car, and the hulking beast that was her keeper followed suit.

"Hey," Jack stammered. The left-hand side of his face was on fire, and the words he got out sounded more like the early babblings of a newborn than the occasionally eloquent wordings of an adult.

The man gave no answer. He did, however, turn to look at Jack. His bald head played host to an angry face with thick, black eyebrows, which slanted inwards with the same level of aplomb as a cartoon villain. His forehead was enormous and his eyes deep set and black. His large jaw seemed to sit directly on his shoulders, for he had no discernible neck holding his head in place. His lips pulled back in a grin revealing golden teeth. He had a large tattoo running across his upper chest. A simple and eloquent piece of body art. FUCK. The font made it look even more graceful.

He sped away before Jack had moved from the spot, and as the car turned at the end of the road and disappeared, Jack lay his aching head back down. He was dizzy from the blow, and his face felt as if it were melting from his skull on the injured side. The heat from the initial strike gave away to a pulsating pain that was close to indescribable.

Jack closed his eyes. His body shook, and in that moment, he was lost. His mind was scrambled, and everything he had fell away and got lost in the fog that was threatening to claim him.

The hungry growls of the approaching undead went some way to clearing the lingering haze. Jack rolled over onto his knees, and raised his head.

The first two pairs of undead hands were reaching for him. Both were largely skinless, the meat already starting to get a dried husk, like when you leave a steak unwrapped in the refrigerator.

Jack walked backwards on his hands and feet, like some strange gymnast, and pushed himself to his feet in a display of strength and flexibility he never knew he had. The two creatures were both wearing the formerly white uniform of a crappy local football club. Their white shirts, now stained with the rusted colour of dried blood, were a giveaway as to their final moments. Even in death, the stench of beer was heavy on their breaths, only now it was seasoned with the odour of early rot.

Jack jumped backwards, unarmed and outnumbered, Jack held no inclination to fight with the two men who each easily outweighed Jack's meagre seventy-kilogram frame. A fresh snarl came from behind him. Jack turned and ducked just as a pair of arms closed in for a hug. A hug that would have ended a little too much familiarity if the flesh-hungry undead freak had had his way. The man was built much more like Jack. His thin frame dressed in the same formerly white uniform of a football club. His head was shaved, which meant there was no way to hide the large split in his flesh that ran from the middle of his forehead, up and over his dome and down to the back of his skull.

Whatever had happened to him, it could not have been pleasant. As he lunged forward, the two flaps of skin lifted and tore a little. Jack had the horrible mental image of pulling the flesh from the skull down either side of the head until it met beneath the creature's chin. He was not sure what good that would do, as it was certainly not going to kill a member of the undead. It was just the image his brain decided to produce.

Instead, Jack chose a more primitive and less hellish manoeuvre, a shoulder tackle. He lowered his shoulder and ran. He hit the reanimated corpse, throwing all his weight behind it.

It hurt like fuck.

He was not expecting the dead to be so unyielding. Later, when he had the chance to reflect, he would realize how stupid that notion had been.

Still, in the moment, he had simply closed his eyes and pushed, casting the slender thing aside and opening up a window for his escape.

Running, his feet slapping against the concrete, Jack looked for an escape. His mind was blank. He had no idea where he was, and even though he had only travelled a minimal distance, he could very well have been in a foreign country.

"Here, over here. Come on, hurry," a voice called him.

Jack stopped and looked around.

"Yes, here, come on, be quick." There was a sense of urgency in the words, which made Jack feel guilty for his lack of speed in locating their source. Looking around, he finally saw movement in a house down the street to his right. Turning, not giving himself time to think, Jack ran.

The house was a middle number in a run-down looking terrace. The buildings narrow but tall, each with three floors, and possibly a small fourth if the owners had been creative with the rooftop area. Jack didn't spend long enough to study their structure to make a judgement. He ran up the concrete steps and barrelled through the front door without as much as a second thought.

He leaned against the wall, his heart racing, sweat pouring from him. He heard the door shut, locks slide into place, and then something heavy rumble as it was pushed across the floor.

Opening his eyes, Jack saw an older man, he must have been in his seventies, heaving a cabinet through the narrow hallway so that it blocked the door.

"Here, let me help you," Jack said, moving beside the man to lend his weight to the effort.

"Thanks." The man had a layer of sweat on his brow.

"No, thank you," Jack answered. He offered the man a smile, but before it could be reciprocated, a heavy thump hit the front door.

"We'd better move back into the kitchen. Come on, my wife has a pot brewing." The man turned and moved with a limp, leading Jack into the house.

The kitchen was warm and welcoming. There was a radio playing, gentle classic jazz music helped to ease away lingering echoes of the hungry dead. The smell of food wafted through the hall and had Jack's mouth watering before he even made it into the room.

"Honey, we have company," the older man said as he walked up to his wife and kissed her on the cheek.

"Well, hi there," the old woman said, smiling. She was older than the man, or at least looked it. Her hair was white and neatly styled. Her face coloured with a gentle flash of make-up, and she was wearing a dress that made it look as if she had plans to head out and attend some summer fete or regatta. "Please have a seat. I am just baking some scones."

CHAPTER 6

Despite his insistence to the contrary, the old couple, who introduced themselves as being George and Mary, refused to let Jack leave the house.

As the day wore on, the undead activity increased, with more and more people falling victim to the sweeping waves of freshly risen dead.

People trying to make a run for it, thinking the coast is clear, were caught unaware by creatures that came from nowhere, moving at a pace that while not a full-out sprint, was certainly more than a mindless amble.

Jack found himself watching the creatures as they came and went. He had eaten his fill of scones, and didn't think he could force another cup of tea down his throat without bursting. Even with the seemingly endless types and flavours the couple seemed determined to introduce him to.

There was a clear difference between the undead. It was all in the eyes, at least, that was how Jack saw it. The undead seemed to have either red or black eyes, and varying shades seemed to indicate something. He just wasn't sure what.

There was a clear difference between the freshly risen dead, those who still had their flesh coloured with the fading heat of life, and those who had been dead for longer. He was impressed that in a little over twenty-four hours, certainly no more than two days, the zombies were showing such distinctive patterns.

"It just doesn't seem real, does it?" George spoke as he moved beside Jack, a fresh cup of tea in his hands.

"No," Jack answered, looking from the man, to his tea, and then back to the scene outside.

A young man who had come sprinting from the right, was taken down by a group of the undead. He had been too preoccupied looking over his shoulder, to see what was right in front of him. They tore through him with such ferocity that his head was pulled from his shoulders and discarded like nothing more than the ribbon decorating the box the gift came in.

"There are differences in them. You must have noticed that," George said, his voice soft, his words slurred a little.

"I was just watching them ..." Jack caught his words. "It sounds so strange to say that. So cold."

"The world will become a much colder place now. Nobody can prepare for this. Nobody can understand what it will take. We are under attack, and the casualties will be heavy. Those who survive will have to change in order to stay alive." There was something in the way the old man was speaking that put Jack on edge.

"What do we do until then?" he asked, looking for advice, for someone else to tell him that it will all be ok.

"We change. The rules of life itself have been altered. So too must we change the rules of living. You must understand the dead. Learn how they work. A body that is freshly dead still seems to be alive, in many ways. Their speed, their strength, it is very much like that of the living. Those longer dead, become stiff with death, rigor mortis, you see. But after twelve hours. That is when the changes really start to happen." George stirred his tea, placed the silver spoon on the saucer and took a long sip.

"How do you know all this?" Jack asked, feeling uncomfortable.

"Death was my business for many years. I was an undertaker, you see. Not that it gives me any advantage or special knowledge. I'm just repeating what I know, and hope that it will help you on your way."

Again, the same ominous feeling swept over Jack, like a shadow over the ground on a summer's day.

George said nothing but took another long drink of his tea. His hands had started to shake.

"I'm not going to survive this new world. There is no place for the elderly. We slow you down." He turned his head and looked at Jack with tears in his eyes.

"What do you mean? You're fitter than me." Jack tried to smile, but the pieces were beginning to fit together.

"Not for long. Find your way to London. Get your girl and make sure you tell her exactly how much she means to you. Every damned day." George reached out and shook Jack's hand. Doing so before Jack even realized he had offered it.

George turned and walked away without saying another word.

"George, George, wait," Jack called, after finding the silence of the room too much for him to bear.

The living room was at the back of the house on the second floor. The kitchen was on the ground floor, along with a small dining room. Jack was moving down the stairs when he heard the first sounds of a struggle. Picking up speed, he hit the small hallway at a run and charged into the kitchen.

"George, you don't have to do this …" he began, but words failed him the moment his brain processed the scene before him.

In his mind, Jack envisioned George killing his wife and then himself. What he saw was quite different. Mary was standing with her hands around George's throat. Her head was tilted to one side. Her lips were pulled back exposing dentures, which had come loose at some point in time. Mary snarled and snapped, as her teeth found George's aged, yet tantalizing flesh.

Without thinking, Jack strode forward and picked up the large cook's knife from the counter top. He stabbed down through the back of Mary's head. The blade pierced her skull with ease, and slid through the grey jelly that was her brain, before tearing through the skin between her cheek and nose.

The body went limp immediately and fell forward against George. The false teeth fell from her mouth and landed on the floor.

George wrapped his arms around his wife and held her still. He said nothing, but kissed her on the forehead and laid her down on the floor.

"It wasn't supposed to be like this." George strained to speak. "The tea was supposed to kill us both. Poison."

"Why?" Jack asked, confused.

"I told you. We are old. Mary has cancer, and I was diagnosed with Parkinson's disease last June. Our days are numbered. Recent events just pushed up the date, that's all." George raised his head to look at Jack. His eyes were stained red with tears. "Don't you worry about me. Go on upstairs. Lock the kitchen door, there is a key on this side you can use. Get some rest upstairs and leave."

As he spoke, George walked towards Jack and helped usher him out into the hall. He placed the key in Jack's left hand, and shook his right one, one last time.

"Thank you, Jack," he said, and closed the door.

Jack stood and stared at his hands, more specifically at the key that lay in his palm. For a moment, he considered just opening the door and walking back inside. He didn't. Eventually, he slid the key into the lock, turned it, and walked away.

The sun was going down and long shadows extended from the shambling creatures who seemed to be milling about in the street. Jack didn't count them, but he guessed their numbers to be close to fifty. On both sides of the street, houses stood occupied. Lights illuminating their windows; providing safety to those inside, while serving as quite the draw for the undead. It was clear to see the houses illuminated with the brightest lights garnered the most attention from the hungry dead.

Moving up to the second, and eventually third floor of the house, Jack looked around. He felt oddly cold as he made his way through the rooms. The bathroom with its tiled walls and dated decoration. A bathtub in place of a shower, and a cupboard with a near endless supply of toothbrushes, mouthwash, toothpastes, and an assortment of medicines bearing both George's and Mary's names.

The main bedroom was a simple affair. A large, old, but terribly comfortable-looking bed occupied the majority of the room. Thick, white-cased pillows and a matching duvet covered the bed. The curtains were pulled back and the warm evening glow filled the room. There was no television, no sign of mobile phones, or anything else modern. A pile of books stood on both nightstands on either side of the bed, and a dresser occupied the far corner. Jewellery and watches, perfumes and aftershaves decorated the top.

Jack took it all in, turning around as he felt the peace of the room wash over him. Then he made the mistake of looking out the window and saw a man fighting off three very lively undead freaks. One of them was using the man's own arm as a club, seemingly seeking to tenderize his flesh before it dug in for its evening meal.

Jack couldn't bring himself to lie down in George and Mary's bed. He didn't know them from Adam, but they had saved him, and they reminded him of his grandparents. Instead, he moved out into the narrow hallway and into the second bedroom.

The room was smaller, but no less comfortable looking. The single bed was decked with the same thick, cloud-like pillows and duvet. Cream-coloured sheets and pale yellow walls; the room was a pastel overload but it worked. Jack sat on the bed, ignoring the chair in the corner of the room. He took off his shoes and looked at his feet on the plush carpet.

"Fists with your toes," he said with a smile. The smile became a laugh, and before he knew it he was lying on the bed with tears in his eyes and a stitch in his side.

Scooting further up the bed, he lay for a while and realized just how fucked up life was becoming. George had been right. The world was changing, and as much as he hated what it was becoming, Jack had no interest in throwing in the towel just yet.

The window looked out onto several other houses, overlooking the rear of the property. The dead were milling about in the street, but that was not what held his attention. The rest of the world did that just fine.

Looking through the illuminated windows across the street, Jack gazed as he saw a woman in the kitchen, cooking a meal. Her husband was at the table with the kids. He could not see what they were doing, but in his mind, he saw them colouring together. One happy family. A few doors down, he saw a woman working out. Her body was jumping and moving, pushing weights around as she kept up with the instructions that played on her television. The final house that he could see had a couple fucking. They were standing up, the girl with her back against the wall, while the man held her there, his hips thrusting.

Jack averted his eyes, not in any mood to spy on someone's fuck session, but it made him smile. The world was carrying on. The world would always carry on. People would always find a way.

Getting up from the bed, he thought about Sarah. She and her mother were trapped, but they were not gone. They too would find a way to survive.

Jack paced the room for a while, unsettled by the strange restful feeling that settled over his mind. He wanted to fight it. He wanted to push it away and go back to the panic and the fear. The uncertainty. It made more sense to him.

Instead, he ran a bath. He had not had a bath since he was a kid, so he made sure to put extra bubbles in it, and make it as hot as he could stand.

The water was close to scalding when he slid down into the tub, but it felt great. He gasped and gritted his teeth as he lay back, his spine moving through the hot water to rest on the still cold interior of the bath.

The lavender-scented mixture in the bath created a soothing steam. As the bath emptied, the water falling below the level of the drainage hole, he would fill it up again.

Jack had no idea how long he lay in the water, but he fell asleep twice.

It was dark when Jack towelled his water-wrinkled body off and slid into bed. He cringed at the thought of putting his dirty

NO ZOMBIES PLEASE WE ARE BRITISH

clothes back on, but the idea of wearing an old man´s clothes, in particular his underwear, was equally unappealing. So Jack was naked when he slid between the sheets.

The bed enveloped him, and within moments, he was taken by sleep. Blissfully unaware, even if just for a few hours, of the continuing destruction of society.

CHAPTER 7

When Jack woke, the sky was no longer dark with the threat of a storm. The sky was cloudless, and a pale baby blue. The sun teasing of an appearance but not yet visible from his position.

He slid out of bed and stretched. The sleep had done him the world of good. Jack looked at his watch and gasped. It was almost eleven, which meant he had slept for thirteen hours straight. He looked around. After studying his blood-soaked clothes for a while, he decided that another man's underwear was not such a bad idea. Dressing in the white bedroom, he found a pair of new briefs, still in the box, and a pair of black jeans that were only a little bit too big. The belt he found by the bed solved that problem, and a black, collared t-shirt completed the look. Socks were also not a problem, but shoes were a different story. Jack didn't mind. His own were more comfortable anyway, and the blood that crusted over them had not yet leaked through to the inside.

Dressed, still feeling relaxed and ready for anything, Jack went downstairs. He paused half way down the final flight. He could hear snarls and growls coming from inside the kitchen. It only took a second for the rested and relaxed feeling to fall away.

Jack stared at the door, knowing it was George who made those noises. He had died, and was now back. Jack debated opening the door and putting the old man out of his misery. It was the least he deserved for his hospitality. Jack couldn't do it.

Instead, Jack moved back to the second floor. The living room had a fireplace. A real, working, wood-burning fireplace. This included a full suite of tools, including a nasty looking fire iron. Jack lifted it from the rack. It was a heavy, old-school iron piece. The handle part of the same single lump of iron, twisted around to give it grip, before ending in a ball to add extra purchase. The business end was a fine point. Six inches or so behind the tip was a large barb that curled from the main shaft and added an extra dimension to the weapon.

Jack swung it in the room, and while it was heavy, he liked the feel of it in his hands.

Any lingering moments of rest and relaxation were blown away when Jack opened the front door and stepped out onto the street. It was early morning, but the freshly bled corpse of a young woman lay in the middle of the street. She was face down, the skin flayed from her body, the bones broken and roughly pushed to one side to allow whomever it was that was so hungry, to feast on her flesh.

The street was littered with the dead, and all seemed to turn at the scent of fresh meat. It didn't take long before Jack got the chance to put his new weapon to the test. The woman came from his left, her mouth dripping with strands of meat. Half of her face was missing, the skin peeled away revealing oddly white teeth along her jaw.

Jack didn't wait for the chance to ask her how the woman on the floor had tasted. He thrust the fire iron in front of him, and stabbed the snarling figure through the throat. Black blood jettisoned from the wound and as Jack pulled the iron free, yanking with two hands, the iron slid so far through the woman's throat that the barb slid behind her neck. Jack pulled his weapon free in an explosion of cold flesh, blackened lumps of coagulated blood and bone. The head lolled backwards, gravity pulling the skull farther back, the flesh tearing more and more. The skull landed on the floor, followed a few moments later by the rest of the woman's body.

Jack stared as the eyes turned towards him, the jaw still trying to chomp down on anything that came close to it.

There was no time to kill the thing because there were two more dead bearing down on him, and another cluster behind them.

Both sides of the street held equally unappealing options, but Jack knew he could not go back inside. He couldn't hide. Closing his eyes for a second, he said what, for him at least, counted as a prayer. He opened his eyes and was already swinging his iron like a club. The skull of the first creature caved inwards, the force of the blow squeezing brain matter out through its nose. The speed of the swing carried on after it fell to the floor. It was then with a backhanded swing that Jack drove the sharp barb into the side of the second dead man's head. The curl slid in through the temple and out through the eye socket. The skull tore as Jack pulled free, placing his foot on the thing's chest to give himself extra leverage.

He was dripping with gore by the time he ran at the second group. Swinging the iron like a man possessed, he struck them down with a series of blows. Only one was a kill shot, but Jack didn't care. The other five fell, and that gave him the window to escape, and that was all he was looking for.

Sprinting down the street, Jack refused to look at what was turning towards him. Jack put his head down and ran. He ran and swung at anybody or anything that came near him. He felt iron and flesh collide and the repeated shower of cold blood as it splattered against him. Everything moved in a blur. Jack had no idea where he was headed, or whom he took down, but by the time he looked up and found himself with enough room to breathe, his arms were numb, and his chest burned so bad he feared he would not be able to draw breath.

His fire iron was bent at the end, and the barb torn off at some point in time. It had been replaced by an ear, which had been impaled on the iron and forced farther down the shaft. Jack let the weapon fall from his hands as he leaned back against the small fence behind him. His hands hardly opened, cramped from holding onto the bar.

Looking around, Jack tried to understand where he was. The street was littered with cars, and a bus sat parked at the stop. The driver stared at Jack, his pale white face streaked with purple veins as he snapped and scratched at the window. Its throat was a mess of torn flesh and dried blood. There were others too, trapped on the upper level, seemingly unable to move down the stairs and out into the world.

Behind him was a children's playground. Jack paused to catch his breath, but quickly turned away. The sight of so many tiny bodies was not something he wanted to dwell on. He saw people staring at him from inside the buildings. Mainly commercial properties. A Pakistani family watched from behind the walls of their shop. When Jack's gaze made contact with them, they disappeared from view.

Others followed suit, hiding or pulling something across their field of vision as soon as they realized they had been spotted.

There was something else too. A tapping sound. Something that had something more behind it than the mindless thump of the hungry dead.

Jack looked around, but there was nobody on the street. Nobody alive, at least.

That was when his eyes returned to the bus. Sitting in the rear, her face pressed to the glass, was a woman. She stared at him, tapping away on the window. Every tap her hand made seemed to further agitate the creatures who were along with her for the ride.

Jack looked at her, and as soon as she realized he had seen her, a smile spread across her face. The relief that washed over her in the moment was so strong Jack could feel it.

He was stuck. He couldn't turn away and leave her.

Bending down, he picked up his battle-hardened fire iron and walked towards the bus. The choice was a simple one. Take out the driver first. It was not as though he would have floored it and driven away with Jack as his new prisoner, but Jack didn't want to get on the bus with that snarling mess still alive.

The driver was a large man in life, and the bloating brought on by the decay had seen him lodged behind the wheel. He strained and snarled as Jack approached, his head crashing against the glass window.

The closer Jack drew, the more agitated the thing became. The glass cracked and split under the pressure of the blows. Softened clumps of rotting flesh smeared the inside, and came close to obscuring the view completely.

Then, with a final strike, the undead bus driver threw his head through the window. Glass shards dug into its flesh, digging deep gouges as the creature shoved its head farther and farther. Jack watched it, a strange, cold fascination growing within him.

He then raised his iron and drove it through the man's head. A single, fluid jab, in one ear and out the other.

What freaked Jack out the most was that from all of the dead he had laid to rest, none of them screamed, or gave any sign of pain. He knew they were dead. That had been a worryingly simple thing to get used to. Yet, their complete silence at the moment of death, not even a gasp as the blow came. That made him shiver.

Moving around the front of the bus, he held the iron at the ready. Adrenaline surging through his body, pushing away the fatigue and muscle ache. There was one other death-walker, but its attention was directed towards the window of the laundrette, which was the building hidden behind the bus. Numerous scared faces looked out at him.

Jack did the decent thing and caved the thing's skull in from behind. He could not do anything to help the people trapped inside. There were three other undead figures making their way through from the laundrette's back room.

"I'm sorry," he mouthed to them.

He knew they couldn't have heard him, unless they were part bat or some other weird shit, so he reasoned that the creatures must have growled at the same moment, for everybody turned around and screamed. They ran around like headless chickens, and before he even had the chance to consider smashing the windows to set them free, it was all over. They had barricaded the front door, but left the rear unguarded.

Turning his attention back to the bus, Jack climbed on board. The stench was atrocious. The odour of piss, shit, and vomit all rolled into one. The high temperature made the aroma all the more stomach-churning.

"Help me," the woman wailed as she saw Jack appear. Above him, he heard the stomping of feet as the undead were driven wild by the temptations below them.

Jack saw why. There was a closed door that ran across the end of the stairwell. A means of keeping the upper deck off limits at certain times, or so he assumed. Not being a bus aficionado.

Then he realized there were way more death-walkers on the bus than he had realized. They filled the stairwell, and he saw the door straining beneath their weight.

"Please," the women cried once more.

Jack raised a finger to his lips to shush her. Even that seemed to bring a fresh wave of tremors to the door. It looked fit to burst.

To her credit, the woman at the back of the bus understood the gesture and fell silent. She disappeared back between the seats, into the place she had no doubt been hiding since this whole thing started.

Moving slowly, afraid to as much as breathe, Jack inched himself deeper inside the bus. He could feel the weight of the undead pressing against the door, and as much as he tried not to do so, he could not help but imagine it bursting, and seeing the horde of death-walkers descending on him.

The door held, however, and Jack managed to move into the back of the bus. A few body parts lay scattered on the seats. Before he reached the rear, Jack found four other bodies, all of whom had been ripped apart in such a fashion that there would be no second chance at life for them.

The stench at the back of the bus changed. Fear was the primary ingredient, body odour and urine being the two underlying scents that created the heady fragrance.

"Hi, I'm Jack." He smiled at the woman.

"Hi," she replied, her voice timid and scared. The sound of their voices brought further crashing and banging from the upper level.

"We need to move, but keep it slow. These things can sense us," Jack whispered, his words barely audible.

The woman nodded in response, her dirty blonde hair flicking over her shoulders.

They got up and moved together through the bus. Jack held his fire iron in front of him while the woman clutched a rather well-used looking backpack.

They got halfway towards the exit when the woman sneezed. It was a small, high-pitched noise, one she tried hard to cover, but it didn't help. The sound sent the creatures into an absolute frenzy. The bus began to rock, and a few moments later, the door splintered and the undead filled the bus.

The woman screamed, and ran back to her hiding place. Jack also retreated, but not before delivering several skull-cleaving blows with his now most trusted ally.

The three bodies dropped and created enough of a barrier in the cramped conditions to buy Jack and his new friend a little time.

He looked around and saw the same faces staring at him from within the confines of their homes and businesses. All apart from those in the laundrette. They were busy being caught in the new in-between state of existence previously called death. They would be back soon enough, Jack was sure of it.

"Why won't they help?" he cried out as he reached the back of the bus.

The first of the death-walkers had somehow stumbled over the pile of its slain brethren. It had fallen to the floor and seemed to show no desire to right itself, instead choosing to crawl along the floor.

"Stay down," Jack said to the woman as he turned around.

He tightened his grip on the fire iron and swung for all he was worth. The window in the rear of the bus cracked but did not shatter. It took two more blows before the glass splintered and disappeared, crashing to the street like heavy raindrops.

Jack went to move, but the crawling dead man had a hand locked around his ankle. Stabbing down, Jack impaled the thing's head on the end of his iron. The creature went limp and Jack was free.

"Hurry, through the window," he called to the woman, who was watching proceedings from the presumed safety of the footwell between the seats.

"I can't," she stammered.

"Now!" Jack yelled, and she moved.

More of the undead were on him, and with the woman moving behind him, crawling over the seat, Jack had minimal room to work with. He stabbed out, but his aim was poor. One creature took the iron through the chest, and two others through the throat. While it slowed them down, it also sent them falling forward, closing the gap between themselves and Jack.

Jumping backwards onto the seat, avoiding the falling trio, Jack stabbed downwards and ended them. He looked around just as the woman disappeared out of the window.

Following her, Jack was almost safe when something clamped down on his wrist. Jack fell forward, his body pulled from beneath him. The fire iron fell from his hands and out of the window. He turned as a snarling, blue-haired elderly woman fell on him. He managed to get his arms up in time, but her weight was considerable, and she was relentless in her endeavours to chew his face off.

Her breath stank of death, and in itself was a potent weapon in neutralizing her prey. Gagging, but not prepared to go out that way, Jack focused himself. His hands were on her shoulders, and he could feel the wounds on her back. The cold, gooey flesh, the jelly-like consistency of the exposed meat beneath. Digging his fingers deep inside the wounds, he tore into her, scooping chunks of decaying meat from her back.

His efforts went unnoticed by the old woman, whose thrashing head was coming dangerously close to making contact with Jack's head.

Straining, Jack couldn't help but roar as he tried to push the woman away, while kicking his legs to fight off the groping hands of the remaining death-walkers, having conquered the barrier that Jack had created.

Jack's strength was waning. He felt the rush of air as the woman's teeth snapped open and shut. He closed his eyes, waiting for the end.

When it came, it was deafening. Blood sprayed everywhere as the bullet tore through the old woman's head. Her skull exploded like a melon meeting firecrackers. Clumps of brain and shards of bone rained down onto Jack.

Jack felt hands grab him and haul him from the window. He felt glass rake over his flesh, drawing blood, which seemed to set the undead commuters into overdrive.

He looked and saw the hollowed-out head of the old woman, crushed under the rush of death-walkers.

His ears were ringing; no other sound came through. Jack's body was limp, his legs barely able to support him. Hands grabbed him, and he struck out, wild and terrified.

Whoever was holding him was prepared for the assault for they evaded his wide, clubbing blows with ease. The hands returned, grabbing at him. They overpowered him, pulling on his arms. He moved backwards, dragged away from the bus that proceeded to vomit death-walkers.

The hands pulling Jack continued to manhandle him, pushing and shoving him this way and that, away from the bus, and away from the dead. A dead figure fell to the floor, a blood-bubbling gash carved into the side of its head, just above the temple.

They reached a building and Jack was pushed inside. He fell to the floor, his ears still ringing with the sound of gunfire. The rest was starting to come back to him, but it was muffled and distant. He looked around, but his vision was failing him. Everything went black. He heard the muffled shouts and screams. He felt the splatter of blood hit him, but then the darkness took hold.

CHAPTER 8

Jack was back home, back in his flat. He heard the screams from his bedroom. He went to jump out of bed, but couldn't. He was tied down. Held immobile by barbed wire bonds, the twisted knots of metal dug into his flesh, burrowing deeper with each jerked movement. Blood ran from his wounds and stained the white bed sheets.

He called out, and the screaming stopped. The door to his room opened and Tania appeared. Anna was in her arms, but she was not the sweet, wide-eyed toddler he had known. Now she was a desiccated corpse. A wrinkled husk of the child she had once been. Tania held her tight against her, unwilling to let her go.

"Why didn't you help us?" she asked, moving forward. "You could have stopped him."

"Tania, please, I …" Jack was silenced when Tania began to weep.

"No excuses. You said you would protect us. You lied to me. You lied to her, and now she is mad," Tania said through her sobs.

"Who is mad?" Jack asked.

Tania did not need to give an answer, for the dried-out corpse in her arms turned its head, the skull rotating one-hundred and eighty degrees on the neck. Anna's leathery skin creaked as it was pulled taut to allow the full rotation of the skull. The eyes opened. The sockets were empty, but that only made the sight even worse.

The Anna-corpse opened its mouth and screamed. A sound akin to fingernails scratching a blackboard. It pierced Jack's skin and made his head ache. His nose bled and his ears burned. He could feel the blood flowing from them.

He struggled against his bonds, but that only drove the barbs deeper into his flesh.

"You could have saved us," Tania said once more before the walls of the room rumbled and shook. Cracks appeared, spreading over the walls. Plaster fell away in chunks until the walls collapsed under the weight of the dead. A horde of rotting death-walkers piled into what had once been a small room. The bodies were dripping with putrefaction. Wet clumps of oozing flesh hung from them in loops, like melted cheese.

They descended on the bed, swarming around Tania, who was holding her daughter's mummified corpse above her head, so she could see the feast as it began.

Jack screamed. He thrashed on the bed, and the barbed wire cut so deep into his skin that it disappeared from view.

Jack woke with the scream stuck in his throat, a hand clamped over his lips making sure it stayed stuck. Panicked, he jumped to his feet, shaken by the dream and the suffocating feeling of being woken up by someone smothering him.

"Quiet, quiet, it's alright. We are safe here," a voice whispered in his ears.

The words were muffled, but audible, the ringing from the gunshot faded to almost nothing.

Jack looked around. He was inside what looked to be a butcher shop. Raw meat lay inside the cabinets, juicy red steaks, and plump chicken breasts. Racks of lamb complete with chefs' hats on the end of each bone. Sausage links lay curled like pythons, and all manner of breaded pieces were stacked neatly. Had it not been for the undead pounding at the locked door, and the decapitated body lying to his right, Jack would have thought he was merely out buying dinner.

"Who …?" he asked, looking around. His eyes fell on the man who clearly owned the place.

"No time for that. Keep quiet. They will leave," he said in hushed tones. He had a thick London accent, which couldn't be tamed even by the low volume.

Jack did as he was told and sat down on the floor. He was next to the dirty-blonde woman he had rescued. She was covered in blood, and sat with her head back against the wall, her eyes closed. She was beautiful. Not in the seeing a girl and thinking she is cute kind of way, but in the out of everybody's league, should only exist in movies and dreams kind of stunning. Her long hair, while thick with grime, still managed to flow over her shoulders. She had a wonderful olive complexion and her features were soft and delicate. Her slender build showed off her ample chest, which stretched the wording of her shirt. Her jeans hugged her legs, and even through the material, Jack could see they were strong and slender.

"My name is Alessa," she whispered.

"I'm sorry," Jack asked, thrown by her sudden communication.

"Me, my name, it's Alessa." She smiled and her hazel eyes shone. "In the bus, you told me your name. Jack, right?"

"Yes, yes, Jack, that's me," he stumbled over his words, feeling more foolish with each syllable he stuttered.

Alessa giggled. "Thank you for saving me," she added. Leaning forward, she kissed Jack on the cheek. It was a friendly gesture, a simple demonstration of thanks. Yet it sent a surge of electricity down Jack's spine.

"You are not from around here, are you?" Jack asked, noting the incredibly sexy accent that she spoke with.

"No, I am from Italy. Rome. I am here to travel, and see the rest of Europe." She stopped smiling.

"I'm sorry you got caught up in this," Jack spoke softly, not sure what else to say.

"Me too, for us all." The smile returned, a fleeting glimpse of it at least, but it was enough for Jack.

The congregation of the undead disappeared from the window in a sudden mass retreat. The screams that rang out a few moments later explained why. They were distracted by an easy kill.

"They won't be back, not if we keep quiet." The man turned around from the door where he had been keeping watch. He held a blood-stained meat cleaver in one hand and a gore-encrusted ball hammer in the other.

The two weapons, coupled with the butcher's bloody apron, certainly created an imposing first impression.

"You are a crazy son of a bitch. Lucky too," the man said as he laid his weapons down on the counter.

"You saved me?" Jack stared at the man.

"I couldn't let you die. Not after what you did to save her." He looked at Alessa.

"You're the only one who thought that way," Jack added, surprised at the level of scorn in his words.

"You can't blame them. People are scared. You've seen what is out there. Not everybody has been able to adjust as quickly as you and me," he said.

"I don't know if I have adjusted to anything," Jack answered him, running his fingers through his hair as he let out a long sigh.

"I saw you out there. You might not know it yet, but you've adjusted. You are a survivor." The butcher cleaned his hands on his apron, adding another layer of black blood smears. "The name is Steve Musgrove."

Jack shook the hand that was extended to him. "Nice to meet you, Steve. I'm Jack, and this is Alessa." Jack tried not to wince as Steve's frying-pan-sized hand clamped over his own. His grip was like a vice.

"You two look hungry. How about we go out back and have some food. As you can see, I've got more than enough, and it is only going to spoil."

Steve led the pair into the back of his butcher shop, through the preparation area. The odour of blood was strong. A coppery scent that lingered on every breath, but Jack found he was no longer repulsed by it. He had smelled enough blood in the previous forty-eight hours for his palate to have become accustomed to it.

They went upstairs into a small living area. An open plan room with a living room, dining room, and kitchen all rolled into one. To the rear were two doors. One leading to a bedroom and the other a bathroom.

"Make yourselves at home," Steve offered to them, ushering them over to the sofa, while he made his way to the kitchen. "Sorry about the mess."

Jack said nothing, but he wondered if the man knew the redundancy of the sentence given their situation.

The flat was sparsely decorated, and clearly with the tastes of a single man living alone. Clothes were strewn not in great numbers but enough to know they had been removed and discarded. They would remain there until being gathered for washing. Beer cans stood on the table, and the reading material was limited to some trade catalogues, a few editions of both Playboy and Penthouse, and a newspaper. Jack stared at it, wondering if there would ever be another paper printed. Was this the final edition of something that would now forever be eradicated from the world?

Jack thumbed through the newspaper, avoiding the magazines; it wasn't right to look at them in the presence of a woman.

Looking up, Jack saw that Alessa was staring at him. She smiled when his eyes met hers, and then turned her head.

Jack smiled, and saw her cheeks flush a delicate shade of red.

"What happened to you? On the bus, I mean," Jack asked.

"I was travelling to the station. I was visiting an old school friend who lives here. They wanted to drive me, but got sick, so I took the bus. We made a stop and ... and this man got on. I was at the back, so couldn't see, but the driver shouted at him, but he didn't listen. He got on and just ... he attacked the driver. He hit him, and bit him. People started to scream, to try to run, but the man was so strong. He attacked them all. There was so much blood. I didn't know what to do, so I hid. I hid and the others tried to hide too. They went upstairs, closing the door to keep themselves safe." She stopped talking, tears in her eyes. She sat still clutching her backpack.

"That's how all the death-walkers got up there. Someone must have been injured, and turned after they locked the door," Jack said, finishing building the scene that he had stumbled into.

"Si, I mean, yes." Alessa wiped her eyes and brushed her hair behind her shoulders. "Is that what they are? Death-walkers?"

Jack smiled. "I have no idea. It's just what I call them. I thought it had a ring to it, you know."

Steve appeared carrying a plate filled with steaks. Too many for the three of them, but as he said, it was only going to spoil.

"We've got rare, medium and well," he said, pointing to the three piles of meat on the platter.

For a while, none of them spoke. They simply devoured the meat, blissfully unaware of how they looked, holding the meat in their bare hands taking tearing bites while juices ran down their fingers and over the chins.

It was to Jack's surprise they polished off the whole plate, and while Steve accounted for a substantial portion of the consumption, it was still an impressive feat.

With their bellies full, they sat back. Conversation was soon needed, for it provided a means to drown out the screams of a dying world.

"I'm sorry." Steve started the conversation by addressing Alessa.

"What for?" she asked, confused.

"For not coming to you. I was … when it happened, I hid. I didn't think. I just hid away." Steve hung his head as he spoke, his shame clear for them to see.

"Nonsense." Jack stepped in. "You came when we needed you. You saved my life, so there is nothing to feel bad about. Right, Alessa?"

"Si." She laughed a little. "I mean, yes. You saved us. You are both very brave."

Jack was watching Alessa talk, and saw her cheeks flush once again, her eyes naturally pulling towards him.

"That's kind of you to say." Steve seemed relieved at their acceptance. "What were you doing out there?"

"Me?"

"Yes."

"I am trying to get into the city," Jack told him.

"Why would you do that? My brother is there. It's even worse than here. Those things are everywhere." Steve looked directly at Jack.

"I have to. My … there is someone there I need to find." Jack didn't understand why he caught his words, or phrased it the way he did. He loved Sarah, she was the reason he was not hiding away in his flat, waiting to be rescued.

"I'm sorry, man, but you won't make it. The army has the city cordoned off." Steve fished around in his pockets.

"So they are fighting back, taking control." Jack heard the optimism in his voice, the hope that things would be over.

Steve pulled out his phone and stared at both Jack and Alessa. "You really have no idea what we are up against." His words were cold, but weren't meant to be derogatory. "My brother sent me this, but I'm warning you. Once you see it, you can't go back."

He held the phone out, and while both Jack and Alessa reached for it, their hands paused for a moment. Were they really ready?

Jack took it, and before he knew it, Alessa had moved over to the sofa and was sitting beside him. She pressed up close, and even though she reeked of death and bodily fluids, a shiver ran down Jack's spine as she brushed against him.

Jack held the phone and pressed play.

The video was shaky, shot from a high-story building and zoomed in to show the ground below, but it was easy enough to make out what was happening. Death-walkers, hundreds of them, maybe even more. They moved along the road like a sweeping plague. People were running for their lives. It was dark, but the lighting of the city showed more than enough. People fell, people were thrown to the lions in order to let others survive. Law and order broke down as panic swept through everything. Those who fell were torn apart, and within three minutes, the video showed the streets flowing with blood. Several of the death-walkers broke away from the pack, moving at a quicker pace. A few even reached something close to a run. They were not going to win any Olympic medals, but for corpses, it was pretty damned impressive. It was also scary as shit, as evidenced by the way Alessa pushed herself even closer to Jack.

As they watched, the police arrived. The riot squads ready to stop the trouble. They were mown down by the wave of gnashing teeth. Their uniforms protected their bodies, but it did not matter where the bite occurred.

The video stopped just as the wave of the undead broke the police ranks and sent the remaining members of the public scrambling.

"That's fucked up," Jack said, nodding in agreement with whatever it was Steve had said before. He couldn't remember it exactly.

"There is one more," Steve told them, his voice grave.

Swiping the screen, naturally moving the wrong way first, Jack found the video and pressed play. The location had changed. It was now on a street view. Steve's brother had big balls it would appear.

The military was there. Not in grand numbers but two armoured four-by-fours with a mini-gun mounted on the back of each.

The camera moved from the guns to the horde and back to the guns again. It then moved back to focus on the people who were caught between. Those fleeing for their lives. A few moments later, the guns let rip. There was no sound, so the first shot was not heard, but the way the bodies danced and twisted as the rounds tore through their flesh, it was obvious what had happened. The camera moved back from the horde to the guns and back to the horde again.

Alessa gasped, and her hand found Jack's, squeezing it tight. The civilians were gone, their bodies lay scattered over the road,

NO ZOMBIES PLEASE WE ARE BRITISH

the red of their blood a rich contrast to the near black excretions of the death-walkers.

The video ended with a freeze frame on the mini guns. The soldiers manning them were stoic-faced, doing their job, and eliminating the threat.

"That was the last one he sent before everything went to shit. That was Saturday night. I think it is safe to say that London has fallen." The words sounded like the title of a dodgy movie, but the sentiment behind them was sobering.

Jack handed the phone back, aware that his hand was shaking as he did it. "I have to try," he said, resolved.

"Your friend is dead," Steve said. "It might sound harsh, but those are the facts."

"No, well, I don't know, but they called me and told me where they were. I have to try, I can't just leave them behind." Jack was resolute in his convictions.

"I will help you," Alessa said, giving Jack's hand one final squeeze before letting go.

"I can't ask you to do that," Jack countered.

"No, but I say it, so I mean it. I will go. You saved my life, I will help you, always." She smiled and that same shiver ran through him again.

"What the fuck, it's better than my plan anyway. You can count me in too," Steve said then smiled. He clapped Jack on the back, a blow that was hard enough to make him wince.

"Why?" Jack asked. "I'm grateful to you, don't get me wrong, but you don't know me."

"I don't. But I did see what you would do for a total stranger. I saw a selfless act, a brave act. You are a leader and thinker. In this new world, we are going to need allies."

"Thank you."

"So what are we going to do?" Alessa asked.

"I think the first thing is a shower. No offense, but you two are filthy, and smell like, well, bad." Steve smiled.

"Oh, yes, showers ... but both ... um, I'm, and she is ..." Jack stuttered, caught off guard.

NO ZOMBIES PLEASE WE ARE BRITISH

"Easy there, Romeo. I have enough water for you to shower separately." Steve came to the rescue.

Jack felt his face burn with embarrassment. Beside him, he heard Alessa giggle. His mind spun trying to find something to say, but he couldn't.

"I'm flattered," Alessa said, planting a kiss on Jack's cheek as she followed Steve. She looked back over her shoulder. Jack was watching her walk. She smiled at him, and he smiled back.

CHAPTER 9

When Jack first saw Alessa, well not the first time, or the second, because she had been cowering in the back of a bus, but certainly one of the first times that Jack really saw Alessa, he had thought she was beautiful. When he emerged from his shower, wearing a fresh set of clothes provided by Steve, he really saw Alessa, and his opinion changed.

Clean, the grime and guts scrubbed from her skin, her dirty-blonde hair no longer quite so dirty, free of the tangles and clumps of who knew what, there was no way beautiful was a word that covered her.

Jack realized he was staring, and felt his cheeks redden once more. "I'm sorry, it's just … you look stunning. It took my breath away for a moment." The flush on his cheek intensified, but an equal shade spread over Alessa's face also.

"Thank you. You look …" She smiled as her eyes ran up and down Jack's new outfit.

Contrary to Alessa's change of clothes, which must have been inside her backpack, Jack looked as if he had dressed himself in the dark.

Alessa was wearing a pair of dark blue jeans, which hugged her figure like a glove, and a long, flowing top with multi-coloured horizontal stripes. Nothing crazy, but blues, oranges, yellows, and browns. It had a wide neck that showed off her slender shoulders, and while it was a baggy top, it somehow seemed to flow over the right places of her body and accentuate them. Her long hair was pulled back into a simple ponytail, which was something that Jack had always found to be a real turn on.

Jack had been given a pair of knee-length cargo shorts and a faded Slayer t-shirt. Both of which were too big for him, and hung from his frame, making him look gangly.

"Yeah, don't say it," he answered, grinning.

Steve rejoined them, having disappeared into his bedroom to change his clothes. "Looking good." He smiled at Jack. "So, the city is about forty-five minutes from here, but I wouldn't expect us to get even half way before we had to duck out of the way and find some shelter." Steve pulled an old road map from the cupboard and spread it on the table.

"How far do you think we could get?" Jack asked. "My girlfriend is in the West End, but I don't know which theatre."

To his left, he felt Alessa withdraw from him, as he finally let slip who it was he was going to rescue.

"I think we could get as far as Holloway, maybe even Camden Town, if we are lucky. Probably have to ditch the car before that, but I know the area well enough," Steve answered, studying the map, pointing to places and marking certain areas with crosses and circles.

"I'm going to leave you guys to talk. I don't know what you are pointing at anyway." Alessa smiled, leaning in close to Jack as she did. He caught a scent of her perfume and his head swam just a bit, only for a second, but long enough for it to add to his confusion.

"Sure thing. I don't have much to offer, but ..." Steve began.

"I'm okay. I will watch the window. Maybe I will learn something." She turned and moved across to the other side of the flat.

"I like her," Steve said, nodding his head appreciatively.

"Yeah, me too," Jack answered, his eyes watching the sexy Italian figure sitting against the window, resting on the slender ledge.

"So, you don't know where your girlfriend is exactly." Steve stressed the word.

"I know, I know." Jack pulled his eyes away and went back to the map. "She was watching a show with her mum. I got a message they were trapped inside, and that all hell was breaking loose. Then I lost her."

"Well, if we can get as far as Camden, we will still have a good five or six miles to cover, and that's not including all the doubling back we are going to have to do. We had better make sure that we mark some places we can stay, crash for the night, or simply for cover. If the military are shooting civilians, then I don't want to come across them if I can help it." Steve studied the map, and added some more marks, this time in red.

"You seem to know what you are talking about," Jack said as he watched Steve work.

"I used to be a music groupie. I would follow the heavy metal bands around with some guys I knew. I would always mark down the itinerary and where we could crash. I figure, this isn't too different. Well, except for the dead wandering around eating us and shit."

It took them several hours to get a plan of where they would move, and where they could crash. In that time, they had several breaks, and were twice summoned to the window by Alessa. Each time what they saw served to terrify them even more, but also confirmed they needed to get moving.

The death-walkers had entered some of the properties, finding a way inside, through the doors and past the barricades. People flocked from their homes, running in fear. They were easy pickings, including the Pakistani man and his family. He was dragged from the shop by his turban, which unravelled as the undead tore at him. For a while, it saved his life, but his escape was halted when two quarrelling corpses ripped his son in half. His tender frame tore down the middle, sending his organs spilling into the road. The creatures descended on the spilled innards, and while they were busy shoving the juicy morsels into their ravenous mouths, the man simply walked towards them and offered himself as their main course.

"We had better stay here one more night. We can each take a watch, just to make sure the place stays secure through the night. Downstairs, in the shop. We should all try to get some rest."

They all agreed, and Jack offered to take the first watch. Nobody argued with him, but as he walked downstairs into the shop, the gloom of twilight casting long shadows on everything, he cursed himself for being so openly helpful.

He sat by the door, having found a nice enough chair in the back office but suitably uncomfortable so as not to promote sleep.

He held the bloody cleaver in one hand, and had the ball hammer lying across his lap. He had cleaned that one up as best he could, peeling away the drying sections of scalp that were still stuck to it.

He hunted around trying to find the gun that Steve had used to end the old woman who had come so close to ending him, but it was not to be seen.

A good thing too, he reasoned. He had never handled a firearm before, but even he understood that using it was a last resort, for it would draw attention to them. It was certainly not a weapon to give a man who sat on the edge of panic, jumping at every bump and scratch that came from the outside.

Evening came and went, and darkness descended. Jack made the decision himself not to turn on any lights. The death-walkers seemed to be largely ignoring the butchers, clearly their nose for flesh only catered to the still living, as otherwise the selection of raw meats would have driven them wild.

There were plenty of screams that rang out, more so as the night fell, but Jack made no move to investigate. There was a time and a place to play the hero, and a fine line between being just that and being a fool.

It was midnight when Steve came down the stairs. He was carrying a thermos can of coffee, and smiled at Jack as he clapped him on the back. They stood together for a few moments. Neither speaking, there was no need. It would only serve to excite the gathered crowd.

Jack made his way back up the stairs, only stumbling once as he crossed the back room. His eyes had adjusted to the dark of the front of the shop, but as he made his way up the stairs, and the doorway closed behind him, the blackness became total.

There were three candles burning in the flat upstairs. One in the kitchen, and one on the table by the sofa. The other could be seen flickering in the bedroom.

Jack looked around but saw no sign of Alessa. Assuming she had taken the bedroom, Jack crossed to the sofa and sat down. He looked out over the road. The street lamps were out. He hadn't even thought of that while downstairs. The darkness was hard-core, yet he could still see them moving around. The world was silent, and it made him shudder. Many of the houses had followed their idea of killing the lights to avoid unwanted attention, but there were more than enough who still had everything burning.

As he sat there, Jack couldn't help but wonder how many of those homes would still be unharmed in the morning.

Movement startled him. Jack snapped his head away from the window. He caught the sound of his shock, but was sure his sudden, jerked movement gave away the image of the cool, calm, and collected man of the group.

"I'm sorry," Alessa said, standing in the doorway of the bedroom. She was holding the candle in front of her. The flame creating a dancing glow that lit up her face and made her eyes light up.

"Oh, no, I'm sorry, I didn't mean to wake you," Jack answered, making sure he kept his voice down.

"I was not asleep. I can't sleep. Every time I close my eyes, I see their faces. The, what did you call them, dead-walkers?" She remained standing where she was.

"Death-walkers. It's kind of a silly name, I know."

"No, it is good. I mean, it's true." Alessa smiled, her lips highlighted by the flickering light.

"You should try to get some sleep. If we are going to do this, then we might not get the chance to rest for a long time," Jack said, while his mind pointed out that if it went wrong, they may all be taking a very long nap in the not-too-distant future.

"I ... I don't want to be alone. Will you join me?" There was a tone of sadness in Alessa's words that made Jack melt.

"Sure," he said, feeling far more nervous than he would.

Moving across the room, Jack followed Alessa into the bedroom. A double bed occupied the centre and a large screen television occupied the main wall. For the rest, there was a wardrobe and a chest of drawers. The room was every much that of a serial single man.

Alessa got onto the bed and slid beneath the covers. Jack followed suit. It was cool in the flat, and the blanket offered a warmth that came closer to a secure embrace than anything else at that moment in time.

The candle flickered on the chest of drawers, casting long shadows through the room.

"Do you think we will make it?" Alessa asked, once they had settled down.

"I do," Jack answered. He was lying stiff, not wanting to relax, and trying hard to ignore the shiver that was becoming a tremor in his body at the mere proximity to Alessa.

"How can you be so sure?" She was looking for a specific answer; Jack was too.

"Because if we don't, we will be dead by this time tomorrow." They were the words that they both oddly needed to hear.

Their situation was not a road trip, not a question of trying and seeing where things led. It was a matter of life and death, a simple equation that changed the rules of the game.

Silence fell. Jack wasn't sleepy, but found a comfort in listening to Alessa's gentle breathing.

"How long have you been with your girlfriend?" she asked, breaking the silence, and making Jack jump just a little.

"A while. She ... it's ..." Jack stammered, trying to find the right words.

"She's very lucky," Alessa said, rolling onto her side to face Jack. "I don't think anybody would ever come and rescue me."

Jack rolled onto his side to face her, their legs and feet touching beneath the blanket.

"Well, I will. If anything happens, I will always come back for you." They both froze. "Steve would too, because we are a team."

Jack felt the shudder as he once again rushed through his words. Alessa smiled at him, her nose wrinkling just a little as she did.

"Goodnight, Jack," she said, and with that, drifted off to sleep.

Jack did not think he would be able to sleep, not anymore, not with the raging torrent of thoughts and emotions swimming through his head, but he was wrong. A few moments after Alessa, Jack followed her into slumber.

When Jack woke, he did so slowly. Coming up from sleep like a swimmer rising back to the surface after a dive. It was smooth, and controlled. He felt awake, he felt alert and rested. It took a moment for everything to filter through. Where he was, who he was with.

He jumped, but kept it a mental reaction, keeping his body still so as not to wake Alessa. They lay together in bed, Jack's body curled around hers. She had her back to him, her body pushing against his. Their hands were clasped, fingers intertwined.

Pulling his hands away gently, Jack rolled to get out of bed. He was as quiet as possible and made it out of the room and into the main body of the flat without causing too much noise. The sun was starting to light up the horizon. The street looked quiet. The undead still milled about, but seemed to be void of any direction or purpose. Jack interpreted this to mean it was all quiet for the rest. They would change that soon.

He got to work in the kitchen making coffee, strong coffee, the way his roommate Terry used to make it. He paused, wondering if Terry was alive, somehow. He hoped so but feared the worst. He was sure that Sue was alive. There was no way even a brainless, flesh-munching member of the risen dead would want to sink its teeth into something as bitter as her.

The thought made him smile and feel impossibly guilty at the same time.

"Good morning."

The voice came from behind him.

Alessa stood in the light of the rising sun, and as she stretched, Jack felt something else start to rise. He turned away and got back to the breakfast. He found a large platter of bacon in the fridge, the power to which was still running. He wondered how long it would be until that all changed and they were well and truly thrown back into the times of old.

"Good morning," he said as he popped as many rashers as would fit into the large frying pan. "Did you sleep well?"

"I did. I feel good." She was behind him, looking over his shoulder at the pan.

Jack wanted to kiss her. The urge was overwhelming; it was staggering in how bold it was. He forced it down. He couldn't. Not yet. They were leaving to rescue his girlfriend. If he were to cheat on her, the whole mission would be pointless. Their near inevitable deaths would be pointless.

"There is coffee over there, but be careful, it's strong." Jack pointed to the coffee pot.

"Strong? I'm Italian," she said playfully and helped herself to a cup.

Steve re-joined them not long after the sun was up and the need for a night watch was over. They ate bacon sandwiches on thick slices of white bread, covered with ketchup and brown sauce. They ate until they were stuffed, enjoying both the company and the meal. They ate because there was no way to be certain when they would have another real meal.

CHAPTER 10

"This has got to be at least ten years old," Jack said.

"Fourteen, but she is reliable as anything you have ever seen," Steve answered.

"Okay, I believe that, but it's an old beast. A diesel too, right?" Jack answered.

"Right," Steve confirmed.

"So it's going to be noisy. Those things will flock to us. Here that might be ok, we could plough them down, but what if we come across a larger group, or they come at us from multiple sides?" Jack hoped Steve would see his point.

The butcher's mobile meat van was parked out back of the building. The street was empty, although a shambling figure in the distance indicated that it might not stay that way for much longer.

"I see your point, but what other choice do we have?" Steve asked, staring at his trusted van.

"I don't know, but we start this bad boy up, they will come running …" Jack left the word hanging as an idea formed in his head.

"What?" Steve asked.

"That's it. We turn it on. We get that noisy engine running and let them come." Jack looked at Steve. He knew he was smiling, and was equally aware it was probably a somewhat lunatic grin.

"I don't … wait, I get it. We bait them with the van, and head out the other way." Steve smiled.

"Exactly. Now let's move it a bit." Jack wasted no time putting his plan into action.

Between them, they moved the van towards the end of the street. Repositioned just short of the crossroads. It was blocking the road, meaning it was exposed on the long side, but also afforded them a degree of cover to make their escape.

"So what do we do? We turn it on and run?" Steve asked.

"If we have to. What do you think, Alessa?" Jack turned around, but Alessa was nowhere to be seen.

His heart froze, and in that moment, his world ended. He looked over at Steve and saw a look of shock and fear on the older man's face.

"Where is she?" Jack asked.

"I don't know. She was right here," Steve said.

"Shit."

"Double shit. We've got company." Steve pointed to the right where two freshly turned, leaking death-walkers were ambling their way.

"Fuck." Jack felt his heart start to race.

Before leaving the shop, they had each armed themselves with a range of large professional knives. Steve held a large meat cleaver and a cooking knife, while Jack had taken a seven-inch boning knife and a ten-inch fillet knife. He also had a ten-inch chef's sharpening steel tucked into the belt of his shorts.

"I'll take care of them. You find Alessa," Steve said, gripping his knives.

At that moment, a car came speeding up to them, coming to a halt just short of running Steve down as he turned to engage the dead.

"What the hell?" Steve gasped as the driver's door opened.

"I knew we couldn't go anywhere in that noise bucket, so I went and found us something quieter," Alessa said, smiling, leaning against the car.

"A fucking Prius, that's genius." Steve laughed, clapping his hands together.

"How did you find it?" Jack asked.

"It was parked down the street," Alessa answered.

"How did you start it?" Jack couldn't help but ask, even as the two death-walkers were closing the distance to them.

"My dad was a mechanic. He showed me a few things when I was growing up. Now, let's go," Alessa said, her voice firm and commanding.

"Yes, ma'am," Jack said as he got into the car.

Steve turned around and buried his cleaver into the skull of the first undead walker and stabbed the chef's knife through the face of the second. Both went down in a crumpled heap.

"Let's go," Alessa said again, impatience creeping into her voice.

"You get in, I'll drive. Just let me get this started." Steve turned back to the meat van and cranked the engine.

The engine growled and spat, stuttering a couple of times before finally roaring to life.

Leaving it, Steve jumped into the Prius, shifted it into gear, and they were away.

CHAPTER 11

The drive was a relatively straight forward one. The roads were largely empty, and while there were groups of the undead meandering through the streets, they paid little attention to the silent car as it drove along.

Steve kept the speed slow and steady, steering the car around the body parts and general debris in a single fluid motion.

By avoiding the motorways and keeping to the smaller side roads, they made good time. Steve seemed to have the twisting and turning roads and tributaries committed to memory, for never once did he stop and show any hesitation as to which way they should turn.

The car was silent both on the inside and the out. Nobody felt the need to talk. Steve looked rather cramped for space behind the wheel, but he did not complain. Jack sat next to him, the knives resting on the dashboard in front of him. Alessa sat in back, watching intently out of the driver's side windows.

From street to street, the neighbourhoods remained largely the same. Residential buildings and a scattering of small businesses and off licenses.

It wasn't until Steve finally brought the car to a stop that conversation was needed.

"Where are we?" Alessa asked.

"Harringray," Steve answered.

"Why have we stopped?" she asked.

"Just down there is Saint Ann's Hospital. You can't see it from here, but it is just down the road. My sister-in-law used to work there," he spoke calmly, staring out of the window, down the street to where a group of the undead had turned their way.

"Used to?" Jack looked at the crowd, which numbered probably close to a dozen.

"Yeah, I guess they don't have much use for her now. You see that thing there." He pointed with one of his large sausage-like fingers.

"A death-walker. Yes," Alessa spoke from the back.

"Yes, well, that's her." The emotion came into his voice. "I guess they were holed up in the hospital. I don't know, but that is her. I'd know her from anywhere." A tear ran from his eye, and he wiped it away.

For a second, nobody spoke. The undead crowd grew closer, their eyes a mismatch of red and grey. At the centre, surrounded by death, was a reanimated corpse whose eyes were as black as night.

"He did it," Steve said, not needing to point for the others to know who he meant.

"They are getting pretty close." Alessa felt the need to point it out from her location in the back seat.

"It's the eyes. The eyes tell it all," Jack began, remembering what George the undertaker had told him. "Red ones and grey ones. I think black means they have been dead the longest. The senior death-walkers."

"Can we move now?" Alessa implored again from the back.

"Yes, yes, sorry," Steve said, pushing his foot to the floor just as the crowd reached the car. They drove away, cresting a hill and leaving the undead gathering behind them.

They continued on for a few moments, before coming to a simple crossroads. Steve looked both ways. Traffic was busier here. Cars stood scattered in both directions. The undead loitered around the stationary vehicles as if they were some shrine to be honoured.

There had been a wreck; a car was lying on its roof, stretching across both lanes. Even from a distance, they could make out the couple in the front seats. Their snarling frames forever locked in place. Farther up, a corpse in cycling gear was crawling along, its mangled legs mashed and caught in the twisted frame of its bicycle. The metal scraped as it dragged along the floor, leaving a meaty trail behind it, like a gore-leaking snail.

"What way?" Jack asked.

"Either way is good," Steven answered him with a long exhalation.

"Both are blocked," Alessa pointed out.

"Then straight on it is." Steve couldn't help but smile. "Let's Die Hard this son of a bitch."

With that, the car took off, mounting the curb with a heavy bounce. It entered the park going faster than they had in a while, and sped off over the grass.

"If we can make it through the Finsbury Park, we can head out around the Emirates Stadium and bring it down closer to Camden," Steve instructed, reciting the place names. Neither Jack nor Alessa argued with him, neither had a good grasp of London geography.

The road through the park was a simple but unstable one. The car held its own on the slick grass, but the trees and other obstacles that came their way made the adventure all the more exhilarating. They swerved around a large group of zombies who looked to have once been a group of powerwalking housewives.

"Watch out," Alessa shrieked as two more death-walkers appeared from behind a group of trees. It was too late to avoid them. Their bodies impacted on the car with a heavy thud. Blood splattered over the windshield as their day-three bodies, bloated with rot, burst.

"That was close," Steve said, firing the water jets to try to clear the window.

"That only seems to make it worse," Jack felt driven to point out.

They drove on, their speed increasing to match the urgency of their situation. The park was a hive of undead activity, from men and women through to children and even the bloated, vein-covered face of an infant, which was peering over the edge of an abandoned pram, snapping hungrily at anything and everything.

Once they had made it through the initial mass of the undead, the car found a wide path that snaked through the grass and around the trees. They came close to losing control as they sped over a bridge that crossed a large stream. A group of people in what looked to be a wedding party appeared just as the car hit the bridge. They were running at a pace, but seeing that they were human, and very much alive, Steve could not help but swerve. The car went off the bridge, but had enough momentum to clear the water and bounce up the bank.

Gunning the gas pedal, Steve pushed the engine and pulled them out of the muddy ground and back onto the path, right into the path of the oncoming bride and groom. The bride was missing her chest, the skin split open so that each unsupported breast was swinging way out to the left and the right. Her rib cage had been opened, revealing the bloody lungs beneath. Her long wedding dress was more scarlet than white, and had a severed foot caught in the train, bouncing along behind her like tin cans attached to the rear of the wedding car.

Her partner was wearing a fitted tuxedo, a steel-blue number that fit his well-built frame perfectly. His jacket was unbuttoned, his dress shirt drenched in gore from the gaping wound on the side of his neck.

There was no way to avoid the pair, and so Steve held the car steady and drove over them. The groom went down, the car bouncing over his body, crushing the bones and bursting the skin like trodden fruit. The bride was not so lucky. She hit the front of the car, her body driven forward so that her face smashed into the metal bonnet. She bounced up and over the car, her skull crashing against the windshield, shattering the glass. She fell into a broken heap on the floor, her dress shredded, her body shattered.

Yet without pausing to examine her wounds, she scratched and clawed her way over the ground towards the stunned and stationary wedding party.

"We should help them," Alessa called from the back. Her face had paled from the sight and sound of the woman's body shattering after hitting the car.

"If we stop, then we are dead," Steve answered.

There was a large group of the undead to their left and an even larger gathering to the right. They were closing in on them, shutting down their exit line through the park. The main road that ran along the park was close, they could see the cars sitting there, abandoned.

"Hold on," Jack said as the car hit the groups closing in. The sides clipped the first few members of the undead party, which must have numbered fifty in total. They were sent flying, legs detaching at the moment of impact, spinning off in another direction with a spurt of congealing, black blood.

"We made it." Jack couldn't help but sound relieved. He turned to look at Alessa, who returned his smile.

"For now," Steve said.

They exited the park and headed east. The road was busy, but it was not blocked. With a little bit of care, they managed to circumvent the traffic and the undead. There were not many on the road, the lure of the park and the fresh meat that it offered seemed to have pulled most away.

They crushed the skull of one death-walker who had fallen from his car and was lying half in and half out.

There was no point swerving, and the already-damaged skull crumbled without even registering a real bump against the car's suspension.

"I'm not sure how much longer this thing is going to hold out. It has taken quite the beating. I've got lights on all over the place, and I don't think any car, let alone a Prius, should be making the noises I am now hearing," Steve said to his two companions, but his eyes were focused on the obstacles before them.

"Then we need to change cars," Alessa said.

"How far is it on foot?" Jack offered, a secondary plan forming in his mind.

"We can look for one, sure," Steve answered Alessa first. "Walking, well, I would say about an hour or so, on any given Sunday. Right now, I wouldn't even want to think." He looked at Jack for a second.

"Then another set of wheels it is," Jack agreed.

The car died on them not much later, conking out in the middle of the road.

"Only one thing for it," Steve said, the reluctance in his voice clear. "Stick together. Let's just keep moving. Find a car and get on with it."

They exited the car, and the first thing that hit them was the smell. The air was heavy with the stench of oil and fumes, but above it all came an odour of death. It was not so much rot, although they were all certain upon sampling the current city odour that rot would soon become a regular part of their lives. This smell was purely death. It was a stale smell. The smell of blood and of final breaths gasped in panic. A stench of bloating and swelling, accompanied by the release of the gasses that caused it.

They moved in a close group. Each of them gripping their weapons in white-knuckled terror. The cars on the road were all either damaged or occupied. The occupants not exactly being open to negotiations, due to their ravenous hunger. A series of lorries clogged the inside lane, their trailers brandishing the logos for everything from food and toys to furniture and clothes. There was also a fish van but it was given a wide berth. The fish inside far from being the fresh produce the van promised.

There was a constant growl around them. It seemed to vibrate through the cars and amplify itself, for there was no sign of the dead themselves. Not too many of them, at least.

A large man wearing a trucking cap came towards them. His belly was swollen to the point where his T-shirt barely covered his navel, not because of death, but rather a life of gluttony. His eyes were burning a deep shade of red and he snarled, his lipless face contorting in what they could only assume was a grimace.

The raw meat that should have been its mouth cracked and wept thick strands of pus as he gave another deep growl.

"Just keep moving," Jack said when Steve moved to dispatch the creature. "He's not the only one around, so let's just focus on getting a car."

They found what they were looking for a while later. Having only come across a handful of death-walkers, only two of which got close enough to require disposal, Jack took out one with a right hook through the temple. Steve dispatched of the second, a larger man wearing biking leathers that seemed several sizes too small for him. His beard had been yanked from his face, swinging loose on a thick flap of bloodied skin, only still attached by a thin strip of flesh on his left jaw.

The four-by-four was sitting there empty and ready for the taking. The keys were still in the ignition. It was as if someone had left it there ready for them to collect.

This was confirmed by the hastily written note they found resting on the driver's seat.

If you find this vehicle, it is yours. Good luck and God speed. The paper was stained with droplets of blood. The presence of a line of three baby seats in the back, each of them empty save for two teddy bears, made for a sobering moment. The chairs had to be removed, and were left sitting side by side on the road. The teddy bears neatly fastened into the seats they had been found in. Alessa had insisted on it.

"We need to get off the road," Alessa said after they had been driving a while. "There are more cars here."

"There is an exit coming up that we can take. It will bring us down and around to head back in the direction we need to be going," Steve said, once again his sense of direction and knowledge of the area trumped theirs considerably.

"Holy fuck," Jack said with a startled yell. "Is that ...?"

"It was," Steve answered, having already seen the site of the blaze.

"Man, that was a sweet-looking stadium. I went to a game there last year," he said as his eyes focused on the burning wall of flame that had once been the Emirates Stadium, home of Arsenal Football Club.

"Mate, I'm a season ticket holder. Have been since I was a kid. It fucking hurts to see that. It really does." Steve stared at the inferno. It was as though the oval roof was nothing more than the mouth of a volcano, the bubble lava it contained ready to erupt at any point.

"What could have caused it?" Jack asked, the flames proving to be a little more mesmerizing than was good for them.

"It could have been anything." Steve stared at the building as part of the walls crumbled inwards.

"Watch out!" Alessa screamed from the back seat.

Her cry pulled their attention back to the road where a man was standing, waving his arms like a lunatic.

Steve slammed on the brakes and swerved the car, missing the gesticulating man by a hair's breadth only to crash into the side of a much smaller and more fragile car.

"Shit," he cursed to himself as he put the big beast into reverse and pulled away.

There seemed to be no real damage to their car, but the one they hit had certainly paid the price.

The man was at the door before any of them could react. His open palms slapping against the windows. His hands frantically grabbing at the handle.

It was only Jack's quick thinking that saved them. He reached over and locked all of the doors, preventing the man from getting in.

"We need to help him," Alessa said as the man pushed his face against the window. Terror widened his eyes and sweat dripped from his face.

"No," Steve answered strongly.

"But –"

"He is hurt, look." Jack pointed to the man's flank. Beneath his jacket, they could make out the torn shreds of his t-shirt and the broken flesh beneath.

"We can't save him," Jack said, looking over at Steve.

It was a wholly unnatural act, to gas the car and pull away from the man. Especially as there were two fresh-looking, red-eyed death-walkers coming up behind him.

They drove away, and while Alessa buried her head in her hands and wept as the man's screams cut above the sound of their car's revving engine, the two men could not help but watch in the mirrors as the dead descended upon the man. Ripping large chunks of flesh from his frame, and dragging him to the floor in amidst a shower of thick blood.

They drove on in silence, not even looking at the continuing scenes of destruction and devastation. Once they circled around the stadium and started heading towards Camden, it became clear that the military had been through. The road was clear; the cars that had presumably been blocking it had been ruthlessly ploughed through, pushed to one side, and crushed under the weight of whatever military beast had acted as the procession's ramrod. Many of the cars had people still trapped in them. It didn't serve well to stop and wonder if some were still alive, alive and unharmed by the dead.

"I think this is where our journey ends, my friends," Steve said as he brought the car to a slow crawl and eventual stop.

"Why?" Alessa asked, leaning forward to peer between the two front seats.

"The military is set up down there. The road is blocked not far up, and behind that you can see them milling about." Steve pointed up ahead of them. Both of Jack and Alessa saw the uniforms moving around.

"So what do we do now?" Jack asked, looking at them both.

"We go the rest of the way on foot." The words spilled from Steve's mouth as if they were the most straightforward and uncomplicated ones he had ever uttered.

"I can't ask you two to do that." Jack was once again struck by the heavy weight of guilt that he was leading these two perfectly kind strangers to their deaths.

"You're not asking. We are offering." Steve clapped Jack on the shoulder and opened the door. "Better look sharp. They probably saw us coming and will have someone coming to collect us soon."

They disappeared from the car, and hurried for the cover offered by the row of brightly coloured buildings. Behind them, a couple of death-walkers appeared from the shadows. They turned and began to amble towards them. Their pace quicker than the recent crowds they had encountered. Their eyes were black and their wounds not as fresh as the others they had seen.

"Quick, in here," Steve said, pulling them both out of the street and through a small alleyway.

A few moments later, a burst of gunfire rang out. Alessa screamed but caught herself. The three of them pressed their bodies against the wall, hidden by the dark. A few moments later, two uniformed men walked by the alley's opening. They could hear the whispered chatter from the two, but they could not make out the exact words.

Steve raised a finger to his lips and pointed. Together, they inched their way to the end of the alleyway. It opened up into the main internal market area. A large sign announcing their entry into Camden Market greeted them. Row after row of empty market stalls sat like skeletons of a time gone by.

The market square was quiet, eerily so. Every sound echoed around in the normally bustling place. Broken windows on the stores inside, showed signs of looting and was the first real indicator that maybe the riots story that had been used as such a masterful cover story had not been a complete work of fiction.

Moving through the stalls, choosing the wider path to take them away from the line of sight of the road, the trio moved on towards the river and the famous loch.

They heard the cahoots and the shouts before the river came into view. Once in position, they could see the problem.

The water level had been taken down. A boat was sitting there, waiting to be brought up, only it was clear to see that was never going to happen. The boat was packed with death-walkers, who stood scratching and snarling at the sides. While above them, on the banks, stood soldiers, or at least men in uniforms.

They were laughing at the dead, throwing scraps of food and general post-riot debris at them.

"That's terrible," Alessa spoke without thinking. Her voice carrying through the abandoned market.

Moving fast, Jack wrapped his arms around her and pulled her away, back into the darkness offered by the location.

None of the soldiers seemed to hear, although the aroma of fresh meat seemed to catch the attention of a couple of the death-walkers, for they turned their backs on the military and resumed their struggle on the other side of boat.

A gunshot rang out. It was followed by a series of hoots and whistles. The soldiers were taking pot-shots at the dead.

"That cannot be the military." Jack looked at Steve.

"I have some ideas, but now is not the time. Whoever they are, they are dangerous, and we need to get away from them." Steve turned away from the loch and moved back into the market.

They followed it a while longer, emerging farther down river, the gunshots and wild laughter faded behind them like a sinister echo.

CHAPTER 12

They walked through the streets, sticking to the back alleyways as best they could. The undead population seemed to be less concentrated here, although as they passed through the residential areas, the growls coming from behind the garden gates told a story that would end quite differently should any of them learn how to open a latch.

"Who on earth were those people?" Alessa asked when they stopped to rest. They had moved at a quick pace and were leaning against the side of a building in a dingy alleyway that smelled worse than any of the undead folks they had met until that point.

"They were the military. What's left of it," Steve answered.

"What do you mean, what's left of it?" Jacked asked through deep inhalations.

"Exactly that. This plague, or whatever you want to call it. I don't think anybody was really expecting it. It caught us off guard. The military too. I think these guys, and maybe those in the city itself, just got caught out. They are trapped and alone, and all they have to keep them sane is the uniform they are wearing." Steve was sweating, his face flushed. He darted his gaze around the alleyway, not stopping to rest for a moment.

"They didn't look very sane," Alessa said, moving closer to Jack.

"It is funny what you can suddenly justify when you are wearing a uniform," Steve told her. "Come on, we can't stop. The day is getting older and we have a lot of ground to cover."

They emerged from the alley and onto a main road. The cars here had also been moved, pushed to one side in an effort to block both sides of the street. To the left and right, cars were set blocking all thoroughfare. There was a cluster of death-walkers in the street, but they had yet to notice the arrival of the trio.

"If we head straight across, that brings us into the zoo. We can cut through the zoo, and jump across out of the park. It's only a short sprint then through to Piccadilly Circus. Finding the theatre your girl is in should be easy, as long as we know the show." Steve looked from Jack to Alessa and back to Jack. His eyes did not have to travel far because the two were stuck close together.

The park stretched out all around them, and the walls of the zoo seemed as tall as those of a castle. Impregnable and imposing as the three stood by the base looking up in awe. The sign for London Zoo stretched out above their heads, and from the inside, the sound of the animals could be heard.

"Here goes nothing." Steve smiled.

"What if the animals ... what about if they are also death-walkers?" Alessa asked as they slowly crept their way towards the main gates.

"I don't think so. I've seen plenty of cats since we set out this morning, and none of them seemed to have turned." Jack surprised them all by answering.

"Turned?"

"Died," Jack corrected himself. "I think animals are immune or something."

The entrance glass was smashed, the barrier turned into a dark maw of jagged shards of glass. Each spike was just as hungry for flesh as the death-walkers that roamed the world. Moving carefully, creeping through the broken glass, not wanting to draw any unwanted attention to themselves, they moved by the empty cashiers' desks and scaled the turnstiles. Inside the zoo, the real world suddenly seemed so far away. To their left, penguins waddled and flapped noisily. The appearance of the strangers rousing them, or so it seemed.

"They must be hungry," Alessa said, stopping to look at the creatures. There were more than a few lying dead, strewn around the floor, both inside and outside the enclosure. "The poor things."

"It wasn't hunger that killed them," Jack said, moving beside Alessa, enjoying the sensation that came with her close proximity.

"The dead?"

"I wish," Jack spoke softly.

"It was the living who did this. The sick fucks. Killing innocent animals," Steve growled, the rage in his words came through like a gust of strong wind.

The two looked at him, knowing that his chosen profession was dealing in animal meat. He clearly saw their joint gaze.

"Being a butcher doesn't make me a hater. I love animals. Always have. I pay more to animal charities every month than anything else." There was no anger in his words when he spoke to his friends, but his desire for them to believe him was strong.

"The living suck," Alessa said, pouting as she bent down to stroke the feathers of a penguin that had waddled up to the walls.

The three walked through the zoo, fully alert for anything and anybody. It looked, for all intents and purposes, that they had the zoo to themselves. It was an eerie feeling, with the animals all reacting to their movements. Growling and crying out for attention and food. There were several bodies lying around, and it shocked Jack when he stopped looking at them. The dead, those ripped apart to such an end that re-animation was no longer an option; headless corpses, bellies bloated to the point of bursting. Skulls cracked open and floating on a now dried-up bed of brain jelly.

They moved deeper into the zoo, alongside a restaurant that had been ransacked. Tables and chairs overturned and smashed, windows shattered. Pools of blood lay amidst a sea of glass shards farther into the heart of the zoo where they found the

Gorilla Kingdom. The gorillas were all outside and seemed to be playing with something. Pushing and shoving it around like a toy. How the death-walker had gotten into the enclosure nobody dared asked, but it was there, and the muscular creatures were manhandling it like a rag doll. While it was still very much alive, even with its bones broken, piercing its skin at all manner of angles, it seemed to have no inclination to attack the animals.

Yet as soon as the group got close, it sensed their arrival and tried to turn and snap at them. The gorillas noticed it too, and a series of shrieks and hoots rang out. It was an awe-inspiring sound. A cacophonous din that made the ground shudder and tremble.

That was when the alpha male showed himself. He strutted out of the complex and into the field, moving through the chorus of yelps and excited barks. He eyed the three newcomers. His dark hazel eyes seemed to shine against his pitch-coloured fur. There was sadness behind them, and a pent-up rage.

He stuck his chest out and walked to the group, to the death-walker that was floundering on the ground like a fish out of water. Without pause, the creature slammed his enormous fist down on the thing's head. It burst like a balloon, showering globs of rotting brain tissue over the ground.

"We need to move," Jack barked, instantly grabbing Alessa's hand. Their fingers locked as if made to fit.

"It won't be able to escape–" Steve began to say just as the large male leaped through the air, catching himself and hauling his gargantuan muscular frame up and onto the edge of the enclosure.

"You were saying," Jack said as they turned to run.

The gorilla stood tall and beat its chest, belting out a roar that shook the glass loose from the shattered windows, while the echo of its chest slaps rumbled like thunder.

"Follow me," Jack called, his grip tightening around Alessa's hand.

Her pace matched his, their bodies close together. They ran along the enclosure deeper into the park, moving past Tiger Pit, where the bodies of at least half a dozen death-walkers lay, dismembered and disembowelled. The stench of their rot was strong, carrying on the light wind.

The tigers stared at them, and nervously paced back and forth.

Turning left when they ran out of room to move straight, they came to a crossroads. The pictographic sign posts failed to indicate a safe hiding place in case of gorilla escape, but they chose to move straight again, heading towards the exit they had planned on using all along.

They didn't get far though, because up ahead of them they saw a group of military figures moving forward, a bunch of struggling death-walkers caught between them.

"Psst. Over here," a voice called out.

It took a moment for them to realize the voice was calling to them.

"Jack, look." Alessa clapped him on the shoulder and he turned his body to stare at the faces peering from inside one of the work buildings.

Not moving, Jack stared at the older man.

"Come in if you want to stay alive," he said, his glasses catching the sun, making it look as if the lenses were winking.

Jack moved, Alessa still glued to his side. Steve followed a short way behind, his gut wobbling, his face a deeper shade of red than they had seen before. Yet, in spite of it all, he seemed to be relatively alert and had soon caught his breath.

Inside the feeding station were five scared people, all wore the uniform of park employees.

Stan Matthews, Ayse Sukür, Richard Whyte, Nathalie Jenkins and Callum Hennessey all introduced themselves in quiet tones, before taking cover just as the military folks came into view. The three newcomers threw themselves to the floor.

The voices of the group could be heard, and the snarls of the death-walkers interrupted them from time to time.

"Are they the same guys from the loch?" Jack whispered to Steve.

"I don't know. I hope so. It's close enough, and they had vehicles, so the timing fits," Steve answered.

"Shh," one of their rescuers spat from wherever they were hiding.

The group walked past, and after a long period of prolonged silence, everybody got back to their feet.

"They come through once or twice a day." Stan spoke first, thus assigning himself as the main spokesperson for the group.

"Why?" Alessa asked.

"To play," Steve filled in. "They feed the death-walkers to the animals, don't they?" He stared at Stan, his eyes burning with hatred for those who mistreated the creatures he held in such high regard.

"Yes." Stan hung his head, his own sorrow equally grand.

"They killed the penguins, too?" Alessa made the assumption.

"Penguins ... don't tell me. I think it is safe to assume you are right. We've not seen anybody else come through in days."

"How long have you been here?" Jack asked.

"Since it started. Saturday, I guess it was." Stan paused as he spoke, calculating how many days and nights they had been cramped together in a stuffy, relatively foul smelling – the relative part coming as a result of being exposed to the open innards of rotting death-walkers – room.

"The riots started not far from here. We didn't know what happened. Everything just went crazy towards the end of the afternoon. They came through in a wave. There was so much panic. People were being beaten, killed, and trampled. Everybody was screaming. It was just ... just ..." Nathalie burst into tears and buried her head on Callum's shoulder.

"You guys cannot stay here anymore. We need to move, to get out of the park," Steve said.

"We are safe here, for now," Ayse responded sharply. Her olive-tanned skin and dark hazel eyes were bright with defiance. She was safe in the food preparation room, safer than being outside.

"Well, maybe not for long. One of the gorillas, a real big bugger, just jumped out of the pen. He's loose around here somewhere. Plus, with those military guys running around, it's only a matter of time before they find you." Steve's words were stern, but he was not angry. It was a voice that would have made him a great father, had he chosen to settle down and have children.

"Where are you headed?" Richard asked.

'We are headed into the city," Jack answered. "Someone I know is trapped down there, and we are going to rescue her."

This response was greeted by a round of nervous laughter.

"I think we will stay here. I'd rather wrestle the fucking gorilla." Callum snorted.

"Fine, but we are moving on. We stand a better chance in a group." Jack stood his ground and stared at Callum. The man tried to match Jack's gaze, but couldn't.

A burst of gunfire rang out, ending their conversation. A window shattered in the building, just two rooms down from them.

Ayse and Nathalie screamed. Richard threw himself to the floor, and Callum stumbled as Nathalie clamped herself around his neck, as good as jumping into his arms.

"We need to move, now," Jack ordered.

He went to leave, but the door behind them suddenly opened and a soldier ducked inside.

He was not looking at the others, in his panic, he was blind to them. With his rifle raised into his shoulder, he peered out of the door. He collapsed a second later. Not even able to force a scream out of his lungs before his head was pulled from his body and thrown against the wall.

The gorilla appeared, filling the doorway. It stared at the people inside and pulled back its lips, baring its teeth.

"Kitaka!" Ayse's voice rang out as she moved to the front of the group.

The gorilla stared at her, its eyes finding hers. The pair stared at each other for a few moments.

"Kitaka, no!" Ayse's voice was strong and powerful. It was commanding and the gorilla took a step back.

Standing to its full height, the gorilla stared at them and beat its chest, snarling and growling.

"Stand down, Kitaka," Ayse said again.

A moment later, the creature's head exploded in a mist of red and grey. The headless corpse remained standing for a moment, before collapsing in on itself.

Jack reacted fast, pushing everybody through the room and towards the back door. They all followed, Ayse resisting at first, unable to break her gaze on the dead gorilla.

The round of bullets that tore into the room got her moving. The group, now eight strong, burst from the back of the feeding area and broke into a run.

"This way, Lion's Den. We can go down into the boiler rooms and double back on them," Stan said as he took the lead. His years put to shame as he sprinted ahead of the rest.

The lion enclosure was a towering and impressive structure. The doors to it were damaged, but seemed to have survived the sweeping wave of violence and death better than many other places. Possibly more due to the occupants of the enclosure than anything else.

"Here, this way," Stan said as they closed the doors.

Another burst of automatic rifle fire rang out and glass shattered behind them.

"Quickly now," Stan said as he fumbled with the lock on a service door.

Yanking it open, everybody disappeared inside, pulling it closed just before the breakaway military group arrived.

"Come out of there. That is an order," a commanding voice rang out.

"That door won't hold them for long. We need to move." Stan led the way through the dark. Grim emergency lighting cast a dim glow that gave them just enough light to see by.

Everybody followed, nobody spoke. They were all scared. The heavy, steady banging of their pursuers as they hammered on the reinforced maintenance door echoed along the bare concrete walls of the service gateway.

The corridor ended, spilling into a workers' area. Tools and equipment lined the walls. A medium-sized tractor mower stood in the corner, and all manner of industrial equipment set lurking in the shadows.

"What is this place?" Alessa asked, looking around her, terror etched into her features.

"It's the zoo's maintenance area. When we built the new enclosure for the lions, it was decided to build a lower level that covers the full area for maintenance. Everything needed to control the park is down here, from gardening equipment to back up security cameras and override controls," Stan explained. He was not even out of breath.

"Will this lead us outside?" Alessa asked.

"Yes. It can actually take us to pretty much anywhere, but we need to act fast because those guys will find a way in." Stan looked from face to face, making sure everybody understood.

"Unless …" Jack said, pausing while everybody turned to face him.

"Unless what?" Callum asked sharply.

"We let them out. The animals, I mean. You said there are overrides down here. What if we just open all the doors and flood the park with them. That should at least buy us some time to get out of here." Jack felt Alessa's hand once again find his own.

He welcomed it.

"This isn't prison," Callum scolded. "It's not like we have a lock down every night." He laughed, but he was the only one. "What?"

"Not every enclosure has it, but lions and tigers do," Stan answered.

"The bears and wolves too," Richard chimed in.

"Can you do that from down here?" Steve quickly moved the conversation along.

"Yes, yes I can. Follow me." Stan set off before he had finished talking.

They followed the older man through the twisting and turning hallways of the underground service area until they reached the sub-level control room.

Stan's pass card granted him access and they entered, nobody saying a word about how he knew what he did, or how he had access to everything.

It didn't take long for him to work his way through the protocols and release all the locks. A siren sounded, and made Nathalie jump. Stan silenced it quickly, even though the echo made it seem as if it were still ringing.

"There, it's done." He rose from the terminal and stared at them all.

They moved on quickly, agreeing to take the first exit back up into the open air. It didn't take long before they found a stairwell that brought them back to the surface. Slowly opening the door, they heard a scream followed by a roar.

Looking, they saw a man in uniform beneath the weight of a giant cat. The body lay still, the gut torn open by the sharp claws that had struck out at it.

"This way." They turned and hurried through the rest of the park, happy to believe the lions and the trouble was now behind them.

"That was close," Nathalie said, rising from the crouched position they had all taken behind the wall that surrounded the butterfly park.

Nathalie's head was broken by a high-powered rifle round before anybody could offer up a warning. A small black hole in the centre of her forehead leaked blood that looked black against her skin. Her eyes stared wide, finishing off her bemused facial expression. She collapsed to her knees, falling face first to the floor.

The first shot was really only a warning. A barrage of automatic fire peppered the wall and had sparks flying like fireflies on a summer evening. Everybody pushed themselves flat onto the floor, Jack and Alessa finding themselves lying face down in the spreading pool of blood leaking from Nathalie's corpse.

The barrage of gunfire continued, a deafening roar that surrounded them. The shots stopped, and the soldiers screamed as another roar rang out. The range of agony-induced screams carried to them, and painted such vivid imagery in their ears that nobody needed to turn around and actually take a look at the scene as it unfolded.

The sound of flesh being torn asunder is a very distinctive one, it lingers in the ears like an echo, only it never fades.

Taking the chance, the group got to their feet and ran. They sprinted in all directions, lost to the panic of the moment. The screams of the soldiers were silenced, which only served to enhance their fear.

Alessa, Jack, Steve, Stan and Ayse all followed a relatively similar path. Three separate groups, but close enough to each other to not lose their way. Callum and Richard were lost.

They saw an exit point and ran to it. Behind them somewhere, a lion roared, no doubt claiming its spot as king of the hill.

The pain came out of nowhere. They were running one second, and the next, Jack felt his leg give way beneath him, a ball of white, hot, searing pain consumed him. He fell to the gravel, dropping like a stone, barely able to bring his hands up to protect himself.

Alessa stopped and screamed. Two soldiers appeared ahead of them, their uniforms stained with blood. Their faces were pale, their lips all but invisible as they snarled. Their eyes had the wide, vacant look of men who had seen the worst and come out broken on the other side.

They walked forward towards the group, eyeing up Alessa as they drew closer.

"My, my," one sneered, licking his lips. "Aren't you a pretty thing?"

"Leave her alone," Jack growled from the floor. Blood was pooling beneath him, as the bullet wound in his thigh went unattended.

The soldiers laughed, and kicked out. Jack took a boot to the face, and all he felt was a rush of dizziness. It surged over him like a rogue wave at the beach, dragging him down and under the surface.

Darkness crept in, threatening to claim him.

He heard Alessa scream again. He tried to move, but another boot sent him down. Just before he lost his battle to stay conscious, Jack heard a rifle crack. He wanted to cry out, but it was too late.

CHAPTER 13

Jack slowly came to. His mind was a mash-up of memories, none of which were clear. He tried to move, but his body ached. Opening his eyes, he looked around. He was in a bed. A real bed. The room was not his, however.

He remembered the zoo. He remembered the gunshots.

"Alessa!" he cried out, forcing himself to sit upright. His goal had been to swing his legs over, get out of bed and find answers. What happened was that a ball of pain shot through him as his head and leg roared their objections.

Jack collapsed back into the pillows and the soft mattress, his jaw clenched and sweat beading his brow as he fought against the agony.

The door to the room opened and Stan walked in. He had a black eye and a sutured gash running along his forehead.

"Good to see you awake. I was worried for a moment that you weren't going to make it," Stan said. "None of us are real doctors after all." He smiled.

"What happened?" Jack asked. Even his tongue hurt.

"Those guys shot you in the leg, and gave you a real kicking. While they were putting the boots to you, your friend Steve appeared. He had acquired a rifle and took the two men out. It really was not as dramatic as it sounds. It was all rather messy and clumsy, really." Stan paused to muse over his words.

"Alessa?" Jack asked.

"She's fine. She was shook up, and thought you were dead. She hasn't left the room since. Just stepped out a few minutes ago to freshen up." Stan smiled at him. "She's a fine girl, you two are good together."

Jack coughed and pain exploded through him, leeching from places on his body that he did not realize could hurt. "I have a girlfriend. She is trapped in the city. That's why we are doing this, to rescue her."

"That may be, but I know that look. The one she gives you, and the one you give her. They can't be hidden, and they can't lie. Trust me, I've been married five times, I know that look. I suck at making it last, but I know the look." Stan winked and lifted the covers to check on Jack's injured leg. "I don't see any infection, so we should be good to get you up and about soon."

"Really?"

"It'll hurt like a bitch, but remember all those dead folks walking around. They won't wait to let you heal up. We've got some good drugs if you want them. Knocks the gorillas right out."

"We're still in the zoo?" The thought terrified Jack for some reason.

"Oh god, no. We are a few streets away. We lugged you to the first house we found. Left quite a trail of blood for those buggers to follow, but we're safe for now. Your buddy Steve, he found the medical rooms and just bagged as much as he could, just in case. He is a resourceful one, alright."

"I'll remember to thank him when I see him," Jack said, groaning slightly.

"You want something for the pain?" Stan asked seeing the look of agony etched into Jack's face.

YES! Jack thought. "No, I don't want to be groggy if we have to move. I think the pain will actually help me focus," he answered.

"Good lad." Stan smiled.

"What about the others?" Jack said as he sat back against the old-school headboard.

"What do you remember?" Stan asked.

"I remember the attack, Nathalie getting shot, and then nothing." Jack tried hard to think of something else. He knew there was something there, but he could not quite grasp it, like the fading memories of a dream upon waking. It remained close enough to tease the mind, but too far to ever offer any answers.

"Well, it all happened fast. Callum and Richard didn't make it. I saw Richard go down, he took a shot through the chest and another to the neck. I don't know what happened to Callum. We never saw him after we split. If he is alive, then he is alone out there." Stan turned and looked out of the window.

"It looks like it is getting dark," Jack remarked.

"It is, you've been out for a day and a half." Stan turned back as he said it, and paused, giving Jack the time he needed to process the information.

"What–?"

"You're awake," Alessa near squealed from the doorway. "I thought I heard you, but I didn't believe it. I thought you were never going to wake." She sped to the bed, ignoring Stan, stopping just short of jumping into the bed beside Jack.

"Hey, yes, I'm awake now. I was just, with Stan." Jack stuttered, Alessa smiled, and Stan gave a loud sigh and walked out of the room, shaking his head and muttering to himself.

"They want to move tomorrow morning, early. They haven't seen anybody outside since we arrived. Nobody alive, anyway." Alessa fell into the chair beside the bed.

"I'm sleepy," Jack said, drifting away.

"It's the drugs. They were strong, and you kept fighting in your sleep. You should rest. Tomorrow, we go to get your girlfriend." Alessa spoke the words with no malice, yet she held Jack's hand within her own, her thumb gently caressing him as he drifted off to sleep.

CHAPTER 14

Jack woke with the birds. Dawn had not yet broken, but the drugs were out of his system, and the throbbing in his leg had torn him from sleep. Alessa was lying on the bed beside him. She had her head resting on his shoulder. Somehow, they had fallen asleep sitting up. They were holding hands, and it took a long time before Jack pulled his hand away, doing so gently so as not to wake her.

It was silent in the house, and yet outside he could hear the steady crone of the undead. It had been five days now since it had first started. The numbers were no longer in their favour. If they ever were.

For the next few hours, Jack sat quietly in the bed, learning to accept the drumming in his leg. He was going to have to if they were going to move today.

He spent a lot of time thinking about the world beyond the house they were in. How many had died? Who had survived? Was there still a government? Had it been restricted to just London? What had caused it? There were too many questions, too many black holes that promised nothing but desolation and fear if you ventured too close.

Jack could feel madness nipping at him like a chasing hellhound. Baying for his blood and soul. Now, in a moment of silence, Jack thought back. Only five days, yet he had witnessed so much loss, so much carnage. His goal had been simple, find Sarah, but now even that had become blurred. With the beautiful Italian leaning against him, nothing seemed so safe and secure, yet so uncertain.

He loved Sarah. He thought he did at least, but now … it was as if the boundaries of his world, which had always been so clear cut, were now nothing but smudged runoffs, like a crayon drawing left out in the rain.

His head ached by the time he heard movement downstairs. Waking Alessa, she stirred slowly. They lay there staring into each other's eyes for just a moment too long; both confused and conflicted. Then Steve walked into the room.

"Oh … oh, I'm sorry." His face reddened.

"No, it's all good, man. We just …" Jack paused, the words failing him.

"I just came to bring you this. You lucked out. Looks like the previous owners left you a gift." He smiled as he produced two long crutches from behind his back. "Weapons and transportation rolled into one."

With a little help, Jack was out of bed, dressed, and on the move. The stairs were a challenge, but he made them unaided, and with minimal pain-sweats.

The house was a well-maintained place, larger than the homes Jack had been in previously, yet modest with its furnishings and interior decorating.

There was no time to spend admiring the place, and no point in planning or discussing decorating ideas, so Jack ignored everything around him and focused on the task at hand.

The power looked to have gone out, and so a large breakfast had been made, cooking as much as the large stove could handle.

People ate, but, if asked, all would have agreed that the meal did not taste of anything. The food was premium, and the cooking perfect. But everybody knew that the loss of power was just one more step towards the future.

Going forward, there would be no more large cooked meals and gatherings. Not for some time at least. When the meal was done, they sat in silence, unsure of what to say. All eyes seemed to gravitate towards Jack.

The streets were quiet, the undead wandered away in search of other prey. The lack of interference made for a smooth beginning to their journey. The gentle *click-clack* of Jack's crutches on the road as he moved had them worried, but there was no other choice.

They were in the city, or what was once defined as it, but you would not have known. The hustle and bustle of the capital was gone, blighted out over the course of a weekend. Terror was heavy on the air, riding on the ever increasing stench of rot.

"Piccadilly Circus is just this way, two streets over," Steve whispered as they stood short of a crossroads.

"It's so quiet," Ayse spoke, voicing the concern they all shared.

"They cleared it out," Jack said, remembering back to the video Steve had shown him.

"Who?"

"The military, or well, whatever they are now," Jack answered. "They swept through and killed everything, and pulled out."

"So they are fighting back, reclaiming the city?" Nobody answered Ayse, there was no need. A few metres farther up, the world answered it for her.

Bodies lay strewn over the streets. Swollen and bloated bellies, stretched to the point of bursting. The formerly undead and the living all thrown to the lions and left to rot where they fell.

The group paused at the sight. They heard someone weeping, but before anybody looked to see who it was, they realized it was them. The tears were unavoidable.

"Do we have to?" Alessa asked as they began to move.

"It is the quickest way," Steve answered. "I hate to say it, but I also think it is the safest."

Nobody could think of any objections, and with the threat of the undead all around them, for while there was no counting the carnage that lay before them, the knowledge they all shared was that it was not enough. It would never be enough.

The actions of the isolated military group had been swift and they had been effective, but not permanent. Many of the shots that were spilled from the mounted guns tore undead heads from shoulders, obliterating skulls and dissolving brain matter in ruthless fashion. However, for every head shot, there were at least as many, if not more, gut shots or limb-severing wide shots, which put the undead on the floor, and undoubtedly killed any living soul that was caught in the blanket sweep of death, but it did not end them. The undead were merely sent to the floor, their hunger unvanquished, the perpetuity of their advance changed but not ended. For the living, their deaths merely acted as a recruitment for those undead that had fallen for the second time.

As such, as the group picked their way through the field of nightmares, there was no way of telling which of the bodies may take a grab at them.

On several occasions, hands or teeth had pulled at Jack's crutches, snatching them from under him.

The group was exhausted by the time they found an exit from the bloodbath, their clothes were drenched with sweat and blood. Their arms ached from the constant downward strikes.

Jack had put his crutches to good use, using them to bash skulls from a distance, and had, when it was all said and done, accounted for a sizable portion of the body count they left behind.

Moving together, as a single unit, it was not long before they were on Regent Street, staring down the long row of tall, pale buildings, and the pillars and rooftop decorations. Over the street, Union Jack flags hung still in the now breathless morning. Their frayed edges and faded colours had taken on a much deeper meaning over the course of a single week. They were a statement, a testament to the strength of the people beneath them. Battered and beaten, they still stood proud, and would not stop until the very stitching that held them together was ripped apart.

The street was empty, save for the bodies, which by now were largely ignored by the group. Nothing more than street debris, stepped over or around, and under certain circumstances, stepped in.

"Is anybody else freaked out by how quiet it is?" Jack asked as they stood in the centre of Piccadilly Circus. The towering electronic screens were as black as the blood spilled from undead wounds. The silence was deafening. It was as if they were the only people on Earth. A fate that all would agree was far worse than being trapped in a world filled with death-walkers.

"Don't say that too loudly," Ayse replied fast.

"Which theatre are we heading to?" Stan asked.

"They were watching the Michael Jackson show," Jack answered.

"Thriller, it's playing at the Lyric," Ayse answered quickly. "What? It's a good show," she added when she caught the looks everybody was passing her way.

Nobody said anything, but for the first time in what felt like forever, they smiled.

"It is down there, on Shaftsbury Avenue." Ayse pointed ahead of them.

They picked their way over the crossroads, the echo of the dead growing every louder. It was almost a welcome relief compared to the silence of the city.

They could see the large poster advertising the show. With their destination in sight, everybody breathed a sigh of relief.

That was when all hell broke loose.

A savage crash from their left pulled their gazes to one side. A tank sat in the middle of the road, swarmed over by the undead. They covered it like a fungus, even hanging from the barrel as they tried to claw their way in. At least a hundred strong were gathered around the iron beast.

Another crash came as the turret spun a little, positioning itself.

"Is it aiming for us?" Stan asked just before everybody threw themselves to the floor.

"No chance. They can't see a thing through that crowd," Steve answered.

Their voices carried, because those at the back of the undead throng turned and immediately focused on the newcomers, egged on no doubt by their intoxicating scent and the primitive craving for raw meat.

They began to move, some fast, some slower, some waddled, their bellies swollen to the point that fluid was leaking through the cracks of their week-dead flesh.

The tank fired a round without warning. A thunderous, ground-shaking roar that decimated a large number of the undead. Those that held onto the turret were blown apart by the force of the blast, their bodies spread over a wide area. Arms and legs rained down on them, and an ear landed on the side of Ayse's head. She screamed and swatted at it frantically, only succeeding in smearing the slime of putrefaction.

They were on their feet before the tank could fire again, the reduction in undead numbers also giving them a few extra seconds to speed towards what they hoped to be the sanctuary of the Lyric.

Across the street, a new sound erupted. A fresh rumble that tore through the auditory spectrum. The blast from the tank had blown a large hole in the building opposite, and as a result, the occupants who had been contained within its walls were set free. Spilling into the world from the jagged gash in the building's flank.

Growls and snarls rang out as the streets filled with the dead.

"Run." The order was given. Nobody knew who it was, or questioned it when it came.

They simply obeyed.

It was not more than a hundred metres to the presumed safety of the Lyric Theatre. Yet never in the history of journeys had such a distance felt so long. To Jack, who was stuck at the back of the pack, his surging adrenaline doing him a disservice by making his crutches more of a hindrance than a help, it felt as if he could have watched all of the *Lord of the Rings* movies in the time it took him to get to the front entrance.

The only thing he knew, was that through it all, Alessa did not leave his side. She could have run ahead, but she stayed by him, with the knives she had taken from Steve's shop clutched in her hands. The once-sparkling steel forever stained with the blood of the undead.

"It's blocked," Stan called out. Noise was no longer an issue. The death-walkers knew they were there, and the groans of the tank as it rolled into view drowned out the sound of their voices anyway.

The tank looked as if it were a living thing, like some piece of *Barker*-horror brought to life, freed from the hills and cities, to roll its way through the capital. Death-walkers clung to their tracks, either hanging on, their desperation to reach the summit outweighing whatever little survival instinct they had left, or their flesh, malleable in re-animation, was stuck between the plates of the tread. One by one, they were rolled along, flipped over and crushed, exploding like grapes, with a shower of guts and innards shooting in all directions. A wet plopping sound, like that of a juicy pimple being burst, was their final contribution in the world.

Still overrun, the large iron monster was turned too late, and in too wide of an arc. It drove straight through the front of the listed buildings that lined the street, and disappeared inside. More pools of the dead spilled out, like vermin fleeing their discovered nest.

"Jesus Christ, let us in. Help, let us in," Ayse and Steve both began to call, hammering on the wood and metal that had been used to block the entrance way. They even hammered on the brick walls, hoping beyond hope that their message would be received.

The death-walkers moved in a flood. The crush of their undead bodies as they spilled from within the buildings was too much for some of the more fragile, rot-bloated creatures. They exploded like overfilled balloons. Strings of cold, jellied intestines and other unidentifiable organs flew through the air like party favours, draping over the lucky members of the closing pack.

The group all pounded on the barricade, and while it gave a little, yielding to their onslaught in a ways that should have given cause for concern to those inside, it did not fall.

Yet.

"Psst, come on, round the side. Quick," a voice called.

The group froze. They looked around and eventually saw a face peering at them from the side of the building.

"Come on, quickly." He waved frantically with his hands, gesturing for them to react with haste.

They did not need another invitation.

The dead were nearly on them, and after Steve turned and took his blades to the first faces of the wave, he too turned and ran, bringing up the rear behind Jack and Alessa.

Steve swung like a madman, hacking at any of the death-walkers that came close enough. Those that he felled served to their advantage, because they acted as a stumbling block for the others.

"Steve, hurry," Alessa's voice cried out.

Steve was surprised to see that the others had all disappeared inside. Taking down one final death-walker with a swinging blow that saw him bury the knife so deep in the creature's rotting skull that his fist was covered in brains, he turned and ran.

Inside the theatre it was dark, and for a few moments while their eyes adjusted, the group was blind and vulnerable.

It was a strange sensation, but once the door behind them was closed and barricaded once more from the inside, the lights came on.

Lights in the form of the torches used by the ushers to move through the theatre in their own sneaky way.

"I was watching you out there. You need to be careful. This place is crazy, those folks … they are … they are dead," the man said, speaking as if he were coming with some grand announcement.

He almost seemed disappointed when nobody panicked or gasped.

"Where is Sarah Welch?" Jack asked. "Is she here? Are there many survivors?"

The man turned around to face the group. "You mean to tell me you actually came looking for this place. You knew what was happening and you came?"

"We did, and we would appreciate it if you would help us. You saved us for a reason, there is no need to play games like this." It was Steve who now stepped forward. "You know what is out there, you have seen what they are. Otherwise, you would not have fortified this place like that."

The man looked at them and laughed. He was an older man, the wrong side of fifty. His hair was cut short and grey all over. He had a white beard growing on his face, which showed he was clean-shaven before the world ended. He smiled.

"We didn't block it because of the dead. We did it to keep out them army folk. They didn't last a day before they started getting all power hungry. They shot a man in the head because he didn't want to get on his knees for them."

"You've been stuck in here ever since?" Jack asked.

"Not stuck, but holed up. They were busy clearing the place and losing their minds. They never realized we were here," the man answered. "I'm Thomas, by the way."

Introductions were made and they agreed to get away from the doors. The dead were gathering outside and they didn't want to extend them an invitation.

They climbed the stairs, creeping in silence, under Thomas's instruction. They did not need to ask why. Behind the locked doors came the suffocating growls of the undead.

"How many of you are there?" Stan asked once they reached the third floor. Once again, he seemed to be the only one of them who was not even a little bit winded from the climb.

"There are six of us left. The rest, well, the rest became those things." Thomas clearly disliked talking about the death-walkers, and it put Jack ill at ease, because it threatened a sense of complacency that would get them all killed.

"You have done well to get them separated," Jack offered, hoping to see some glimpse of triumph in Thomas's eyes. All he saw was pain.

"We ran," the older man said. "We just kept climbing higher and higher. If they break through again, then we have nowhere left to go." They were not the words of a fighter, but of a man who had given up.

"Then why did you save us?" Steve asked. "If you don't think you have anywhere left to go, why save us?"

"To give you whatever extra time we could." His answer was short and it was simple.

"Come with us, we are not staying here." Alessa took her turn to speak. "We just came to find Sarah."

Jack looked over at the young woman who so confused his thoughts. She spoke of his girlfriend as if she were a friend of hers.

"Sarah?" The question in his voice made Jack's heart sink.

"Sarah, she is five-four, blonde hair, green eyes, slim build, friendly but a little distant, too." Jack watched the man's face for any sign of recognition.

"I know her, didn't know her name was Sarah though. I thought Sharon, hmmm." The man turned his back on them and entered the theatre.

It was dark; the upper section of the once beautiful Victorian-style performance house was dominated by shadow. The sound of the dead chomping at the bit in the sections below rolled in the stale, rot-heavy air.

The survivors sat together, side by side in the middle of the upper tier. The sole attendees for the last show on earth. They turned around to look at the group of newcomers, but none spoke. Jack searched the six faces and there, in the middle looking at him without so much as a trace of a smile on her face, was Sarah. She was pale, and her hair was dirty and covered with grime. Her lips were puffed up and the lower one was split on one side, but there was no denying it was her.

"Sarah," he said, struggling to find the right emotion to use.

"Hi, Jack. You shouldn't have come here," she answered dismissively.

"Why, Sarah, we came to rescue you, all of you," Jack began, but the words tasted stale. He had come to rescue Sarah, but that desire had died, the trip was no longer about that, and they had never given any thought to rescuing anybody else. Even Sarah's mother, who he saw then was not part of the group.

"Really?" The scorn was there for all to see.

"Jack, man, they've given up," Steve whispered to Jack. "Look at them."

Jack could see it, each of the six survivors had the same dull look to their eyes; a listless expression and that just screamed surrender.

"Sarah, come on, did you really think I would leave you behind?" Jack began, feeling his cheeks flush with embarrassment.

Sarah burst into a hateful laugh. Below her, the undead were far more interested in the goings on in the upper seats than in the lifeless corpses that lay on the stage, or those that stood trapped in the band pit, their instruments crushed and tarnished at their feet.

"Jack, I'm sorry," she said with a sudden clarity in her eyes. "I ... I never expected any of this to happen, but I also didn't expect you to come chasing after me."

"I don't get it." Jack felt Alessa tense beside him. She took a step forward.

"You were cheating on him," Alessa growled, her voice angry. "You were not here with your mother, but with your boyfriend."

"Sarah, what the hell?" Jack moved forward, and at the same time, a muscular, dark-skinned man rose from the chair beside Sarah.

"Who the hell is this?" Jack pointed at the man, his heart thundering in his chest. He stared at the man and felt nothing but hatred. He balled his fists.

"Now, I know what this looks like ..."

Jack strode forward, his fists raised and before the man, who was considerably larger, could react, Jack threw a right hook that caught him on the jaw and knocked him backwards. He followed it up with a strong left, thrown without finesse but backed by a rage, the purest of all emotions. He felt the man's nose explode beneath his fist, and felt the warm blood coat his fingers.

"Jack, stop!" Sarah screamed, but it was to no avail.

Red mist descended, Jack looked on, as if he were standing beside Steve. He watched as his own body gave in to rage. Everything they had been through, everything they had fought for. His world and everything he had based it around was gone. Destroyed by an unfaithful girlfriend and her big black lover. Jack's fists moved in a blur, and blood splattered his face and his hands. Lips turned to mangled lumps of flesh, teeth knocked out or through, deeper into the skin that surrounded them. Jack roared as he rained down hammer fists, further shattering the man's nose and closing his eyes beneath a swollen mass of flesh.

"Jack, Jack." Shouts and screams rang out as members of Jack's group moved to pull him off, while Sarah lunged at her now ex-boyfriend, her fingers hooked into claws; savage talons that were feral and eager to taste blood.

"Leave him alone." Alessa's voice rang out as a shriek, rising above the clamour of the rest. She lashed out with a kick that caught Sarah in the ribs and sent her crashing off course into the barrier of the upper tier.

Sarah hit hard, her hands raised in attack, she had no time to brace herself. She paused for a second, turning to stare at the others, a trickle of blood ran from her lips. Then she was falling, toppling backwards.

"No!" Alessa cried out, sprinting over towards the woman she just struck. She arrived just in time to watch Sarah's body crash against the siding of the second tier. Her spine snapped with an audible pop that seemed to rise up to Alessa's ears. Her folded-over body then fell down into the first-class seating, where it was as good as caught and torn apart by arguably the best-dressed death-walkers in town.

Alessa turned. Everybody was staring at her. Even Jack had gotten to his feet, the man on the floor no longer recognizable. He was still breathing, but his survival in the new world depended on a lot more than just the ability to draw breath.

"Jack ... I ... she ..." Alessa stuttered, her body trembling as she spoke.

Jack said nothing, but he looked down at the man on the floor, and to his hands. His fists were still balled and blood dripped from his knuckles.

"Everybody stop!" another voice roared. "What the heck has happened to us? Are we no better than the savages down there?" a man said, from the row of chairs. He was old and shrivelled, his balding head and hanging jowls gave him a look that made Jack think of the images of Winston Churchill. He stood, using a black cane to support his somewhat considerable bulk. His body shook through ailments rather than fear, but his eyes were clear and his voice authoritative. "We are still people, this is still England, and I would expect us to remember that."

Beneath them, there was a rumble that was followed by a snapping sound, like twigs breaking in a forest.

"What's that?" Ayse asked.

"I believe they have escaped," the old man answered, taking his glasses from his face to clean them with a handkerchief before replacing them carefully. "Now would be the time that we show a united front." He began to move through the seats and surprised them all by being the first one out of the theatre.

The group followed him, a clear rift in their numbers, but at least they all headed in the same direction.

"Here they come," one man announced, as if the rising tide of death needed to be pointed out.

"To the roof," Jack called, pointing farther down the hall where a sign indicated roof access.

Jack's group turned and moved, sprinting to what they hoped was safety. They stopped and turned as they reached the door. The dead consumed the others. Only the old man was standing tall, surrounded by death. One by one, people disappeared through the door, until only Steve and Jack remained. They watched the man as he struck at the death-walkers with his cane. Knocking them fiercely on the head before they overwhelmed him. He never made a sound as they tore into his gut and swallowed his insides while his heart still beat.

CHAPTER 15

Closing the door to the stairs, they rose, climbing them to the top where they reached a ladder that led to the roof.

Jack and Steve arrived to find Alessa waiting for them. The hatch was open, Stan and Ayse were disappearing through it. The cool rush of fresh air was welcome. None of them had realized how stuffy it was in the theatre.

"Jack, I …" Alessa began, but Jack stopped her. He took her and pulled her into his arms. They hugged, and while they did, Steve took the chance to move to the roof after the others.

"Now isn't the time. We will need to talk, but let's get out of here first." Jack smiled and wiped away a tear that had rolled down her cheek.

The roof was wide, with sections that rose and fell, but it was predominantly flat, with enough room for them to move around.

"Where do we go from here?" Stan asked.

"Guys, come look at this," Ayse called. She was standing on the edge of the roof.

"You guys go ahead. I'm good right here," Steve quickly offered.

Jack and Alessa moved over to Ayse. They looked over the edge of the building and saw the street below. It was a seething mass of the undead. Death-walkers crammed the street like the start of the London marathon. They flowed from buildings into others and back out again like a flood.

"What the hell? Where did they come from?" Jack asked.

"This is London, they came from here," Ayse answered. "This thing is just beginning."

"And you don't know the half of it," a new voice called.

Everybody jumped. They turned, and one by one, their eyes fell on the man standing at the back of the roof. Then they saw his uniform, and lastly, the automatic weapon he held in his hands.

"Who are you?" Steve asked.

"My name is Ryan, Ryan Cosgrove," the man answered, not moving, making it difficult to judge if his weapon was going to be pointed in their direction, or if they could ignore it.

"Were you part of that group down there?" Jack took a step away from the ledge.

"I was, but I don't want any part in what they are doing." Ryan, too, took a step forward, and swung his rifle over his shoulders.

"What is it that you want?" Jack resumed his questioning, hoping the relief he felt at seeing the rifle disappear did not come through in his words.

"I guess the same as you. To get out of here. To leave the city behind and find somewhere to settle down and rebuild." He and Jack both reached the middle of the roof, and the two of them became the stars of the show.

"Rebuild. You mean–"

"You mean it's spread farther than London? Was that your question?" Ryan interrupted. "Shit, you guys know nothing. It's everywhere, the whole country is down. Britain is gone. It was wiped out overnight."

"What caused it?" Steve asked.

"What about Italy?" Alessa could not help but ask.

Ryan looked at Jack, their eyes locked. They communicated the way men do, one leader to another, for unbeknownst to him, Jack had in that moment been cemented as the leader of their pack. Ryan nodded at Jack, a gentle almost imperceptible movement of the head, but it said everything that needed to be said. Ryan then looked to the others. He saw their faces; the fear, the anger, the glint that told him they were survivors.

"We don't know exactly what caused it. It would seem that that initial shock was an airborne transmission, but now is not the time to discuss it. We need to move. This building is no longer secure." Ryan turned to his right and pointed. "We can make it to the other buildings, and scurry down the street without having to hit the floor. There was a roadblock set up down there. It won't give us much time, but it will help us gather our thoughts before we move out. Ma'am, I don't know about Italy. France is gone. Those things were coming through the tunnel this morning. That was when we shut it down."

"So where do we go from here, once we get off the roof, I mean?" Jack asked.

"That's not my call. You're running this show, boss. You tell me." Ryan stood down and offered his loyalty to Jack.

Jack froze. Everything was happening too fast. He had never thought his plan through, because he never thought it would actually work. He never thought he would survive long enough to reach the theatre. Not once had he planned on what came next. He knew it was foolish, but that was simply the way it was.

"We need to leave the city. We can head north, as far as we can go." Jack turned to address the others. Ryan stood beside him, and Alessa and Steve moved over to them.

A few moments later, Stan and Ayse joined the group.

"What do we do once we get to where we are going?" Ayse asked. "If these things are everywhere, then what do we do?"

"We take it one day at a time. We fight, and we survive, and then, when we find the right spot, we will start to rebuild. We are not the only survivors. There are others out there. Plenty of us. We will retreat, and we will regroup, and build the world back up," Jack said, feeling the energy of the group lift his spirits. He also felt Alessa's fingers searching for his. He opened his hand, and her palms slid down against his own, their fingers interlocking once more.

The groans of the dead echoed through the ransacked London streets, but on the roof of the theatre, a new hope had been born.

THE END

CHECK OUT OTHER GREAT ZOMBIE NOVELS

RUN
by Rich Restucci

The dead have risen, and they are hungry.

Slow and plodding, they are Legion. The undead hunt the living. Stop and they will catch you. Hide and they will find you. If you have a heartbeat you do the only thing you can: You run.

Survivors escape to an island stronghold: A cop and his daughter, a computer nerd, a garbage man with a piece of rebar, and an escapee from a mental hospital with a life-saving secret. After reaching Alcatraz, the ever expanding group of survivors realize that the infected are not the only threat.

Caught between the viciousness of the undead, and the heartlessness of the living, what choice is there? Run.

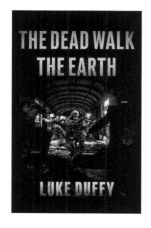

THE DEAD WALK THE EARTH
by Luke Duffy

As the flames of war threaten to engulf the globe, a new threat emerges.

A 'deadly flu', the like of which no one has ever seen or imagined, relentlessly spreads, gripping the world by the throat and slowly squeezing the life from humanity.

Eight soldiers, accustomed to operating below the radar, carrying out the dirty work of a modern democracy, become trapped within the carnage of a new and terrifying world.

Deniable and completely expendable. That is how their government considers them, and as the dead begin to walk, Stan and his men must fight to survive.

CHECK OUT OTHER GREAT ZOMBIE NOVELS

VACCINATION
by Phillip Tomasso

What if the H7N9 vaccination wasn't just a preventative measure against swine flu?

It seemed like the flu came out of nowhere and yet, in no time at all the government manufactured a vaccination. Were lab workers diligent, or could the virus itself have been man-made? Chase McKinney works as a dispatcher at 9-1-1. Taking emergency calls, it becomes immediately obvious that the entire city is infected with the walking dead. His first goal is to reach and save his two children.

Could the walls built by the U.S.A. to keep out illegal aliens, and the fact the Mexican government could not afford to vaccinate their citizens against the flu, make the southern border the only plausible destination for safety?

ZOMBIE, INC
by Chris Dougherty

"WELCOME! To Zombie, Inc. The United Five State Republic's leading manufacturer of zombie defense systems! In business since 2027, Zombie, Inc. puts YOU first. YOUR safety is our MAIN GOAL! Our many home defense options - from Ze Fence® to Ze Popper® to Ze Shed® - fit every need and every budget. Use Scan Code "TELL ME MORE!" for your FREE, in-home*, no obligation consultation! *Schedule your appointment with the confidence that you will NEVER HAVE TO LEAVE YOUR HOME! It isn't safe out there and we know it better than most! Our sales staff is FULLY TRAINED to handle any and all adversarial encounters with the living and the undead". Twenty-five years after the deadly plague, the United Five State Republic's most successful company, Zombie, Inc., is in trouble. Will a simple case of dwindling supply and lessening demand be the end of them or will Zombie, Inc. find a way, however unpalatable, to survive?

CHECK OUT OTHER GREAT ZOMBIE NOVELS

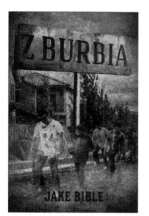

Z BURBIA
by Jake Bible

Whispering Pines is a classic, quiet, private American subdivision on the edge of Asheville, NC, set in the pristine Blue Ridge Mountains. Which is good since the zombie apocalypse has come to Western North Carolina and really put suburban living to the test!

Surrounded by a sea of the undead, the residents of Whispering Pines have adapted their bucolic life of block parties to scavenging parties, common area groundskeeping to immediate area warfare, neighborhood beautification to neighborhood fortification.

But, even in the best of times, suburban living has its ups and downs what with nosy neighbors, a strict Home Owners' Association, and a property management company that believes the words "strict interpretation" are holy words when applied to the HOA covenants. Now with the zombie apocalypse upon them even those innocuous, daily irritations quickly become dramatic struggles for personal identity, family security, and straight up survival.

ZOMBIE RULES
by David Achord

Zach Gunderson's life sucked and then the zombie apocalypse began.

Rick, an aging Vietnam veteran, alcoholic, and prepper, convinces Zach that the apocalypse is on the horizon. The two of them take refuge at a remote farm. As the zombie plague rages, they face a terrifying fight for survival.

They soon learn however that the walking dead are not the only monsters.

Printed in Great Britain
by Amazon